ALWAYS

Catherine Sellers

A KISMET™ Romance

 METEOR PUBLISHING CORPORATION

Bensalem, Pennsylvania

For Bill, for encouraging me to be all that I can be,
for believing in me when I doubt myself,
and for loving me, even when I'm not loveable.

With special thanks and much love to the Condors.

CATHERINE SELLERS

Catherine Sellers was born and raised in Texas, but, as the daughter of an oil field roughneck, she never stayed in one place for long. Now settled with her own family near Beaumont, Texas, where she worked with her husband as an insurance agent for five years, she is finally doing what she loves best—reading all she wants and writing full time.

ONE

Jared Sentell leaned over the steering wheel, his forehead furrowing as he squinted to peer through the rain-splattered windshield. The headlights sliced through the darkness and driving rain, but his vision was still too distorted to really make out the blurry shape walking toward him on the opposite side of the one-lane road.

"What the hell . . . ?"

He slowed the pickup to a crawl as he neared the figure he could now see more clearly: It was a woman, alone except for what appeared to be a small animal clutched to her breast, walking toward nowhere because this road dead-ended at the clay pit.

Braking to a stop, he lowered his window just enough to call out to her. "Hey, lady—" The wind threw his words right back at him.

She didn't respond, but plodded past him without a glance. Planting one foot methodically in front of the other, she staggered along, as though the act of taking the next step was her only goal in life.

Watching her painful progress, he swore softly.

"Damn." What was the matter with her, he asked himself, and where had she come from? She wasn't there just twenty minutes earlier when he'd come this way searching for downed fence and stray cattle. And he hadn't passed a single car since leaving his ranch over an hour ago.

He threw the truck into reverse and eased backward until he was alongside her once more. She pressed onward, oblivious to the rain pelting her face and the wind whipping her skirt about her muddy legs. Something wasn't right and he wasn't about to just drive away. He backed up again, this time far enough so the headlights bathed her in light.

Setting the emergency brake, Jared pulled his Stetson lower over his forehead, then opened the door and bounded across the dirt road in four long strides. So intent was the woman that she didn't stop until he stepped directly into her path. Still, she didn't look up. Reflexively, Jared followed the line of her gaze. All he saw was his own mud-splattered boots standing opposite her small bare feet. Slowly, mechanically, she raised her head. His breath lodged in his throat as her lifeless stare seemed to bore straight through him.

They stood looking at each other for what could have passed for an eternity, but in reality was only seconds. Even in the semidarkness and though bruises and blood marred the delicate features of her heart-shaped face, Jared recognized an ethereal beauty few women possessed. And yet it was her eyes, unseeing and transfixed, that haunted him.

Then she spoke, the tiredness in her voice touching him as surely as the wind and rain. "Are you going to hurt me, too?" Pitifully direct, her question was barely a whisper.

"Christ!" He quickly removed his denim vest to cover the tattered remnants of her blouse. His fingers brushed her bare shoulder. She recoiled at his touch, dropping her handbag in a fleeting moment of awareness.

Easy, Sentell, don't frighten her even more. He went down on one knee to retrieve her purse. Glancing up, he felt that he would drown in her vacant stare. Suddenly it occurred to him how threatening he must have appeared towering over her. He remained on one knee in the mud.

"No, angel. I only want to help, if you'll let me," he said with more calm than he felt. He had only a moment to marvel at how easily the endearment had come before a faint mewling sound drew his attention to the flurry of movement clutched tightly to her breast.

The kitten in her arms struggled to be set free; its claws dug into the tender flesh of her shoulder. Jared flinched involuntarily at the sight of blood trickling from her wounds—and yet he knew she wasn't aware of the pain.

"Let me have the kitten," he coaxed softly. "Come on, give it to me." She hesitated briefly, then handed the wet, wild-eyed animal to him.

Jared settled the kitten into the crook of his arm and held out his free hand to her. "Everything's going to be okay now." He made a concerted effort to speak in soft, even tones.

Uncertainty creased her forehead and Jared sensed she was judging him. He knew also that he was in for a fight if she refused his help; he had no intention of leaving her alone in the middle of nowhere. He waited, scarcely breathing, for her to respond. At last she reached out, her small hand trembling with the effort, to take his hand.

When their fingers touched, he couldn't describe what he felt. He only knew for certain that standing in the darkness on a rainy spring night some vital thing inside him had altered, a change so subtle, yet so complete that his life would never again be the same.

Moments later in the cab of his pickup, Jared glanced at the woman huddled in nerve-racking silence against the door. If only she'd cry or scream, anything but that damnable quiet. He'd seen it before in Vietnam: the outward calm, the zombie-like movements, when the mind couldn't cope with reality.

Reality.

Unconsciously his grip on the steering wheel tightened. Consciously he suppressed the impulse to reach out and comfort her, to protect her from any more harm.

She struggled to open her eyes. Bright lights and loud voices intruded into the darkness that had mercifully shrouded her during the long drive.

Leza Colletti rolled her head to one side, but it hurt more than she could bear. It was so *hard* to think. What was wrong with her? She glanced around again, this time more slowly. Where was she and why couldn't she remember how she'd gotten here? She thought harder, trying desperately to recall anything, any detail that might give her a clue. There was something, a vague recollection of . . . what? People. Lots of people, shopping, browsing . . . A flea market? She squeezed her eyes shut, as if she would be able to summon all the answers by thinking hard enough. But she was unable to recall even one tiny shred of the last few hours, and the realization crystallized into a knot of fear.

Mustn't fall apart, she cautioned herself, and tried to calm the panic she felt by concentrating on the ceiling and counting the light fixtures, one by one.

Cold. She was incredibly cold.

White-clad nurses scurried by, but only one took more than casual interest in Leza. She stopped, glanced at the clipboard someone handed her, and spoke reassuringly.

"You're going to be just fine, Lisa—"

"Lee-za," she interrupted weakly, automatically stressing the long "e" so many people mispronounced. "My name's pronounced Lee-za."

"So it is," the nurse said after double checking her records. "Now, can you tell me if you're allergic to any medications?"

"No. I mean, yes I can tell you, and no I'm not allergic to anything."

The nurse jotted something down on the chart, then handed the clipboard to the orderly at the head of the gurney. "Number twelve," she told him and smiled down at her patient. "Someone will be with you soon. We're a bit shorthanded tonight. There was a six-car accident on the loop earlier. Try not to worry." With a gentle pat on Leza's shoulder as she readjusted the blanket, the kind nurse was gone.

Accident? The word echoed inside Leza's head. The gurney continued on through the corridors, jolting her painfully when it careened around the corners. Surely, if she had been in an accident, she'd remember. But she didn't, and that worried her more than the pain that racked her body at every bump and turn.

With supreme effort, she turned her head to look at the curly-haired orderly maneuvering her stretcher. But it was the other man who caught her attention. Tall and lean and dressed in western clothing, his long-gaited stride enabled him to keep pace with the gurney. He looked familiar, but she didn't know him. Or did she?

At last they reached their destination: A door marked simply 12. Inside the room, the orderly wheeled Leza to a halt, then locked the wheels into place. After helping her to the examination table, he turned to leave, but pulled up short when he encountered the tall man in the doorway.

"I'm sorry, but you'll have to wait outside."

Another chill struck through Leza. She didn't want to be alone. Perhaps she didn't know the man, but his presence was oddly comforting. She was glad he made no move to leave.

The hospital attendant did not share her feelings. "Are you a relative?" he asked, an air of authority icing his question.

"No."

"Friend of the family?"

"No," the other man said without hesitation.

"In that case you'll have to wait outside."

"*You* wait outside," the taller man shot back and pushed his way past the dumbstruck orderly to take a seat in the only chair in the room.

"Listen, mister, it's against hospital rules—"

"Rules be damned." The man smiled at Leza. An instant later his smokey-gray eyes darkened to frosty charcoal when the orderly started to protest.

Three people were in that room and three people saw it was useless to discuss it further. The orderly left in the stony silence of defeat, closing the door behind him.

Alone with a man she didn't know, in a place she didn't recognize, Leza felt suddenly quite vulnerable, utterly afraid.

"Try to relax. Everything's going to be okay." The velvet timbre of the stranger's voice was a warm caress in a cold, sterile place, a balm to her wounded psyche.

"How can I relax?" Leza scarcely recognized her own shaky whisper. "I have no idea what's happened to me."

"There'll be time for all that later. Right now, what you need is rest and medical attention."

She attempted to return his reassuring smile, but again the pain was too much. She winced and turned her gaze slowly back to the whiter-than-white ceiling.

The room grew deathly still. The muffled sounds of

hospital life on the other side of the door emphasized her isolation. For the first time since waking, Leza felt a prickle of irritation. In the past ten minutes, two complete strangers had told her not to worry and had assured her that she was going to be just fine. How did they know for certain? She sighed heavily. Had she slipped somewhere along the way into the Twilight Zone, a place where everyone she met knew all there was to know about her, but where she knew absolutely nothing about anything? She suddenly felt light-headed, and nervous laughter bubbled dangerously close to the surface.

Magnified by the stillness in the room, a faintly audible sound drew her from the realm of near hysteria. Water dripped from the vee of her self-appointed protector's hat to form a puddle on the shiny, waxed floor. One drop splattered between his mud-caked boots, then another, and another.

"Is it raining?" she asked, not certain he'd heard her until he answered.

"Yeah, for a couple of hours now."

She knew he was watching her even though she dared not look at him. Her gaze wandered about the room, then came back to rest on his hands. Cowboy hat and boots were definitely his style, she noted, not so the dainty straw handbag clutched firmly in his large, sun-browned hand.

"Clashes with the boots, doesn't it?" he said with a smile that almost made her forget her troubles momentarily. Grateful for his lighthearted attempt to ease her mind, she smiled back. But her smile disappeared when she realized it was her bag.

How had he come by it, she wondered, and why was he with her now? She closed her eyes and took a deep breath, consciously gathering the strength to think this all out. What had happened? Why had her mind blocked out the past few hours so completely? Everything was so strange. She knew her name, the date, even the details of her background: She was Leza Colletti and today was April third. She had lived in Odessa all her life and now she had a new job in Rosemont, Texas, where her brother lived. Why, then, couldn't she remember anything about why she had awakened in a corridor just minutes earlier? Again her eyelids drooped from the effort of trying to piece it all together. It was all too much for her to cope with now. She was simply too tired and oh, so very alone.

The thought of the home and the family who had always been her strength triggered memories of happier times, and of the love and trust that could take away the hurt and fear.

Leza forced her unfamiliar surroundings from her mind, and thought back to the cozy study that held a wealth of cherished memories for her. She remembered the many times as a child that she had hidden under the monstrous mahogany desk to lie in wait to "scare" her unsuspecting father, only to be enfolded in a laughing, growling bear hug. She could almost see him sitting there in his huge, overstuffed wing chair, a fire blazing in the fireplace at his back, the smell of his pipe tobacco clinging to every book, every piece of furniture, and to him. She would miss those long, quiet talks, the times she'd shared with her father, and most of all the closeness between them.

Tears prickled behind closed eyelids as she lay on the hospital examination table, alone in a room with a stranger, and relived the last few moments she and her father had shared in their refuge from all pain, all disillusionment . . .

"You don't have to pull up roots and move clear across Texas just to prove you can control your own life," Michael Colletti had said, beseeching his only daughter to reconsider what he felt was a rash decision.

Leza could see the hurt he fought to hide and moved across the room to kneel before his chair. Unlike her older brother Steven, who had rebelled against everything their parents had tried to teach them, Leza had always been an obedient, respectful daughter. It was difficult now to stand her ground, to do what must be done.

"I know, Dad, but it's best this way," Leza said with gentle conviction. "You and Mom have been wonderful since Amy's death." The ache in her breast was intense. It had been only six months, and she, of course, still found it difficult to deal with the death of her two-year-old daughter. A rainy night. A drunk driver. A senseless accident that had left her baby in a coma for days before finally dying, and her ex-husband guilt ridden for being alive. Leza forced back the tears that always came with the memories.

"But, Daddy," she continued, instantly regretting the use of her childhood name for him. He looked more vulnerable than she'd ever seen him. "I can't stay here forever, letting you and Mom take care of me. And more important, I can't let you keep feeling sorry for me. I'm almost twenty-seven, and I've never really been on my own. This new job is a godsend for me. I'm going to take it." She hadn't meant to sound so emphatic and her father's hurt expression made her choose her next words more carefully.

"Just be happy for me. Randolph's is probably the finest department store in East Texas, and I was up against some pretty stiff competition." She couldn't help the smile of satisfaction that spread across her face. "And I'm finally going to get to do what I do best—visual display at a store that promises as many outside projects as I can handle. Besides," she reasoned, "Rosemont isn't that far away. It's not like I'm moving to a foreign country where they speak a different language and I don't know anyone." Michael Colletti's resigned grimace almost made Leza laugh.

"Might as well be," he'd muttered. "Over four-hundred miles and eight hours of hard driving."

"But now you'll have a reason to take some time away from the office," she said with the impish grin that never failed to win her father over. But the grin died a sudden death when he didn't smile back. Leza dreaded what she knew was coming. She had never been able to fully explain to her family the reasons behind her divorce. But she knew that today was the day she was going to have to try.

"I just don't understand what happened between you and Don, Sunshine. I thought the baby would make everything all right between you."

"Not even a child as beautiful as Amy could keep me with Don." Leza's voice was bitter with the memories of the many arguments Amy had witnessed. "I know you and Mom kept hoping we'd reconcile, but there simply wasn't any going back. I couldn't live with his . . ." She searched for the right word. ". . . possessiveness any longer. And he'll never change." Even knowing she'd been justified in her decision to leave Don, Leza couldn't help the sense of failure that washed over her. "And poor little Amy. What we put her through before . . ."

He pulled her onto his lap then and wrapped his arms around her, comforting as only a father can. She'd snuggled closer, burying her face in his shirt front until he pulled back to look down at her.

"Don't you go feeling guilty for the way things were. It couldn't be helped and can't be changed." Leza watched him, knowing intuitively the control it took for him to say those things to her. Not once in her life had she seen this strong-willed man admit defeat. For him to finally accept the loss of someone as precious as Amy was monumental.

"That's why I don't want you to leave us now," he broke into her thoughts. "You need us more than ever. I can't bear the thought of you alone way out there." Still a handsome man, Michael Colletti suddenly looked older than his fifty-four years.

"I won't be alone. Steven has room for me until I can find my own place." Leza was the one giving comfort now and for the first time she realized that her father was no longer young. It was vital she make him see how important this move was to her—without diminishing his role as her protector.

"I'll always need you and Mom, but . . . I don't remember ever making a major decision on my own. Mom understands. I wish you could, too," she said.

"All right." He relented, cupping her chin and looking down into eyes that were the same unusual shade of blue as his own. "I have no choice, now do I? But why does it have to be so soon? Your job doesn't start until next month."

"It's been a rough year for me, Dad. I need some time to myself." She had to choose her words carefully, had to make him see her side. "This trip can be a break, a long overdue vacation. I can do what I want, when I want, with no schedules to follow and no one to answer to." She hoped she was getting through to him. "I can do some sightseeing, maybe a little shopping, then have the rest of April to get settled before going to work." She breathed easier when he took her hand and squeezed it.

"Promise you'll call if you need anything . . . anything at all." He'd spoken so softly Leza was certain it had been to cover his emotion. "You'll always be my little Sunshine."

Clinging to each other, feeling the same desperate need to express their love, Leza inhaled the tobacco-y, masculine smell and whispered, "I know, Daddy, I know . . ."

Leza's universe whirled erratically, combining bright lights with vivid medicinal odors that almost gagged her. The room, with its placid green plaster walls, became a swirling sea of unfamiliar sounds. Had this all happened before? What was going on?

"I think she's coming 'round," a voice, fuzzy and devoid of any real emotion, rang in her ears.

Distorted shapes came into sharp focus, then faded again. Something cold and unyielding probed between her thighs.

"Good, we're all through here," a deep disembodied voice replied. The sound of metal clanging against metal reverberated inside Leza's head. "Get her out of the stirrups and for Chrissake let that cowboy back in here before he goes on another rampage."

Hospital, Leza tried to reason. *I must be at the hospital.*

"Amy?" She choked the name from her dry throat. "My Amy, is she all right? Where is she?" Disoriented from her mental wanderings into the past, Leza had lost all sense of time and place. Images of her lively blonde-haired daughter filled her mind, leaving an empty void somewhere in the region of her heart.

"Who's Amy?"

"I don't know. She was alone when I found her."

She knew that voice. He sounded so anxious, so caring.

Other voices, distant and hollow, filtered in and out just as a pleasant, pain-free darkness slipped over her.

"Mrs. St. Clair!" the first voice worried her back to awareness. "Mrs. St. Clair, can you hear me?"

No one had called her Mrs. St. Clair since . . . since the divorce . . . since Amy's death. Her heart filled again with the devastation of the car accident, the long sleepless days and nights in the hospital, the funeral—all piercing through the numbness that had settled like a protective shell around her battered body.

"Where am I?" Leza asked as her head cleared.

"You're safe now, Mrs. St. Clair. You're at the Medical Center, and after we've treated your injuries we'll take you to your room."

"Injuries?" Leza glanced from one unfamiliar face to another until her eyes came to rest on the enigmatic stranger in the doorway. Of course, now she placed him. He was the man in the rain.

Ignoring her obvious confusion, someone whose nametag identified him as J. King, M. D., continued, "But first, Mrs. St. Clair, we'll need some information for the police report."

"Police report?" Leza parroted, wishing he would stop calling her by the name she'd discarded after Amy's death.

"Are you presently using any form of birth control?" he asked, his eyes never leaving the chart he continued to scribble notations on.

"What?" Leza blinked in dismay.

"We have to know these things for your own protection. There's always the chance of pregnancy and disease. Now, when was the last time you had sexual relations?"

"Preg . . . what are you saying?" Leza hadn't meant to shout and was startled by the sound of her own voice.

"Try to stay calm." The man in white signaled the nurse standing quietly in the background. Leza didn't see her coming until it was too late and the sting of the injection had pricked her numbed senses.

"What . . . was that?"

"Just a little something to calm you." Sensing a movement behind him, the doctor placed his body between Leza and the man he'd referred to earlier as "that cowboy." "Can you tell me the date of your last menstrual period?" Misinterpreting her hesitation for shock, he hurried on without giving Leza an opportunity to answer him. "Really, Mrs. St. Clair, there's absolutely nothing for you to be concerned about. From the pelvic examination, I can assure you that there should be no future complications. The cervix is engorged, which tells me one of two things: You were either pregnant before the assault tonight or it's time for your period." His voice droned on and on and Leza wanted to scream at him to shut up. "In any case, I'm giving you something which should determine within twenty-four hours whether or not you're pregnant." He'd barely spoken the words when another stinging sensation burned Leza's hip.

Dr. King made final notations, then handed the chart to the nurse. "It isn't uncommon for victims of a sexual assault to block the entire episode from their memory."

Sexual assault? Leza couldn't believe what she was hearing. It wasn't possible. She'd remember if something like that had happened, wouldn't she? From the corner of her eye, Leza saw the man by the door stiffen.

"The memory loss won't last long. Most women are able to put the unfortunate incident behind them and lead happy, normal lives."

She opened her mouth to speak, but the words seemed to have lodged in her throat. Could he be right? She couldn't remember anything since leaving the flea market, but her clothing was muddy and torn, her body a mass of bruises and scratches. Had she been raped? *Oh, please don't let this be happening*, Leza prayed, but then something the doctor had said earlier dawned on her.

"Did you say I was at the Medical Center?" At his affirmative nod, Leza felt sick inside. "In Rosemont?" Again he confirmed her fears.

No! she railed inwardly, struggling to get up from the examination table. Steven worked at Rosemont Medical Center. *He mustn't find out. No one must ever know.* She sat up, ready to bolt from the table, but two nurses standing nearby moved to restrain her.

"Please, Mrs. St. Clair, you'll hurt **you**rself," one nurse tried to reason with her.

From nowhere, it seemed, the cowboy in the doorway interceded, taking Leza into the protective circle of his arms.

"Shh, it's all right," he whispered reassuringly, his large hand cupping the back of her head.

"Please!" Leza wailed against his chest. She could feel the effect of the drugs draining the fight from her. "I can't stay here. He'll find out if I stay. Please." Gazing up at the man holding her, Leza saw no threat in his anxious face or in his eyes, which were the color of deep, tarnished silver. She'd heard a saying that a person's eyes were the windows to their soul. If that were true, she knew she could trust this man, and she gave herself over to his care.

"Please don't leave me."

His heart hammered against her cheek; his voice was a gentle rumble in her ear. "I won't leave you, angel. I'll take care of everything."

TWO

Jared stood quietly at the foot of his king-size bed. Not for the first time in the last few hours, was he disturbed by the emotions stirring within him. She seemed even smaller and more helpless in sleep than she had in the emergency room, and all he wanted was to lie beside her, protect her from the memories he knew would return all too soon.

"Damn." His curse was an exasperated whisper in the stillness of the darkened room. What sort of madness was this? In retrospect, he realized that he had reacted irrationally at the hospital. He also knew that he had no choice once he recognized the fear in her eyes. Whatever her reasons, the thought of being admitted to the hospital had been as frightening to her as not knowing what she had faced alone on that dark country road.

Absently raking his fingers through his hair, Jared deserted his protective post to open the French doors leading to his balcony. There he stood, shoulder braced against the railing post, watching dawn creep over the horizon with the age-old promise of a new and beautiful day. The dampness hanging in the early morning twilight did little to dissuade the antics of a family of rambunctious blue jays flitting from one sprawling live oak to another.

In the distance, silhouetted against a backdrop of mauve and red and deepest blue, the movement of several dozen head of cattle meandering toward one of many stock ponds dotting the landscape caught his eye. He breathed in the fragrant blend of fresh air and blooming foliage from the garden below, and took visual inventory of his beloved Summerset. From the carefully planned orchard of majestic pecan trees and thousands of acres teeming with a vast herd of Charolais, to the fine old farmhouse painstakingly renovated to its present glory, Summerset Ranch was indeed a reflection of the man who had built it all—stately, imposing, proud.

Again he let his gaze sweep all that was his, and waited for the swell of accomplishment that never failed to fill the void within him—a void he had refused to acknowledge until that very moment. He raised his eyes heavenward and for the first time questioned his reasons for struggling so relentlessly to build his fortune. What did any of it mean when he felt more empty than the cloudless Texas sky overhead? And why, he wondered with no small amount of irritation, this sudden, absolute sense of futility when at age thirty-eight he had achieved every goal he'd ever set for himself?

Unconsciously flexing both fists against his thighs, Jared was suddenly consumed by a rage so intense that it was hard to contain. But then anger had never been a stranger to him, he realized, swallowing the acrid bitterness that always accompanied thoughts of his childhood. Injustice angered him. Stupidity angered him. Cruelty angered him. The vicious assault on the woman now lying in his bed had been all three, but was his anger truly aimed at the man responsible—or at himself for caring more than he wanted to admit?

A faint noise drew him back into the shadows of his bedroom, saving him the ordeal of further self-analysis. She had turned in her sleep, spilling her ebony mane across the pillow. The ice pack had relieved some of the swelling, and not even the bruises on her face or the slightly swollen lower lip could detract from the delicate features he had memorized. In that instant, Jared had a mental image of her face alive with a smile, with eyes bright and clear without the haunting emptiness he would never forget. Her laughter would be pure and sweet, capable of capturing a man's heart as innocently as her beauty.

Sunlight filtered into the room while he studied her. His gaze followed the gentle outline of her heart-shaped face, the pert, slightly flared nose, and the artfully arched brows above thickly fringed lashes. She was pretty, he had to admit, but he had known more beautiful women. So what was it that drew him to her? He resisted the urge to swear again as he rationalized his feelings of responsibility. He had, after all, found her wandering aimlessly on his property. And what man wouldn't feel protective under the same circumstances?

Compelled by a need he didn't understand, Jared moved to stand beside the bed again. No longer was she a nameless ragamuffin; she had a name, a past, a future. Leza Angelique St. Clair. He mulled the name over in his mind. Yes, he decided, it suited her. He eased down to sit beside her and did what he'd wanted to do for hours—he touched her, first her hair, which yielded softly to his fingers, then her hand. There was no wedding band, but there had been no money in her purse either. Both could have been taken during the attack. The only identification in her purse had said she was from Odessa. What was she doing so far from home?

Without conscious thought, he brushed away a curly lock of hair, his fingertips lightly grazing her cheek before caressing the gentle curve of her jaw with the back of his fingers. It wasn't important, he decided, and tucked the sheet protectively around her shoulders. He would find out later. What was important was that she was finally resting—and that she was here.

She tossed fitfully, her whimper breaking the silence before she settled back down. Even in sleep her expression was tight, guarded, and drew out his incessant need to protect—a need Jared didn't dare examine too closely. If he did, he would have to question his motives for every action he had taken since finding her.

Mentally he reviewed them: He had stubbornly refused to leave her at the emergency room door, even though he knew she would receive the medical attention she needed. He had, as a matter-of-fact, behaved like the schoolyard ruffian when the orderly had tried to send him to the waiting room. And why, he wondered with a scowl, had he put her in his bedroom? There were four others he could have chosen. Maybe it was because something vital to his well-being had been missing all these years? Maybe it was to remind himself he had been fighting nature by deliberately excluding the one thing essential to his fulfillment as a man? That choice had been his, he knew, but other people had also influenced him.

Intellect told him not to judge all women by the two who had almost destroyed him, but a deeper voice of self-preservation bid him caution. He had learned years ago not to disregard intuition, and instinct warned him that this woman had the power to finish the job the other two had started.

Christ, wouldn't Jake get a charge out of this! Jared could almost hear his twin's booming laughter: *God*

Almighty, little brother, you've really let yourself in for it this time!

Confused by emotions held in check for so many years, Jared cursed and abruptly stood. What the hell was the matter with him? No woman had touched him this deeply since—

Again he swore beneath his breath. *Damn them both to hell for all the pain.*

With determination born of frustration, Jared stalked to the door. He didn't need this kind of self-abuse. After all, he hadn't consciously chosen to become involved with her. She was just some poor, unfortunate waif he'd been obliged to help. Any other man would have done the same. Hell, he was as much a victim of circumstances as she was, he told himself. Yet, he caught himself glancing back at the small form nestled in his bed and was struck by the futility of his arguments. At any rate, he'd find out more about her and about her family, and once she was physically and emotionally able he'd send her packing. She was trouble, pure and simple. He could feel it. Things were just fine the way they were. He didn't need her around to complicate his life—or share it—or cause him any heartache. Yes, soon she'd be gone, he vowed, ignoring the rush of regret at his decision.

But the memory of vacant aquamarine eyes and a shaky voice asking *Are you going to hurt me, too?* simply could not be ignored.

The shrill ringing of the telephone died in the middle of the second ring. Jolted awake, Leza rolled over to stare groggily at the clock on the night table.

"Five forty-five," she groaned at the digital display and pulled the sheet over her head. Why had she set the alarm for such an ungodly hour? "Just thirty minutes more," she bargained with herself.

She yawned and stretched beneath the sheet, breathing in the faint, unfamiliar scent of aftershave. The spicy aroma was at first pleasant, then alarming. Things weren't connecting in her brain. The alarm hadn't gone off and if she'd requested a wake-up call, wouldn't the motel operator have let it ring until she answered?

Leza pushed the sheet back and looked around the room, slowly trying to orient herself to her surroundings. Nothing was familiar, but then why should it be? One motel room was about the same as the next, and she'd certainly seen her share since leaving home over a week ago. Still, something gnawed at her, something intrusive and frightening. Why was everything so vague . . . so dream-like? And something about the light was all wrong.

She shook her head in an effort to rid herself of the drug-induced fog that had settled over her. Had she taken one of the sleeping pills Dr. Walker had prescribed after Amy's death? That would explain the surrealistic memory of floating up a long flight of stairs. Had her befuddled mind conjured up the shadowy figure who helped her with the bath she insisted on, then gently placed her in this very bed? No, she chided herself and, with a nervous gesture, brushed aside the riot of curls that fell across her forehead. There was no reason to let her imagination run rampant. Things like that happened only in books or movies. Why then couldn't she shake the perception of a presence in the room with her throughout her restless night?

This is crazy, she thought, and sat up to make a slow point-by-point inspection of the room. Her eyes widened apprehensively. Large and bathed in sunlight from twin sets of French doors, this was not your common, everyday motel room. From the sumptuous moss-green carpeting that blended perfectly with luxurious drapes and a matching bedspread of green and beige, to the huge four-poster bed dominating one entire wall, it was decorated to express only one person's preference—tasteful, expensive, and decidedly masculine.

The panic Leza had managed to control since waking began to build at an alarming rate. How had she gotten here? Where was her luggage? She tugged at the fresh smelling T-shirt that had twisted around her body while she slept. And she didn't see her clothes anywhere.

She scrambled from the bed, every muscle in her body screaming in rebellion as she looked for her belongings. Her search came to an abrupt halt the instant she caught a glimpse of her reflection in the dresser mirror, a reflection she barely recognized. With trembling fingers, she touched the puffy slit in her lower lip and winced at the soreness there.

"God, no!" Leza's hoarse whisper filled the room. She stepped back and lifted the T-shirt to expose more of her legs. Stifling another outcry, she stared in disbelief at the bruises and scratches between her thighs. She raised the shirt higher, and what little strength she had deserted her. The sight of the clearly defined imprints of large fingers on her breasts forced her to slump heavily onto the chair beside the dresser. Tears wet her cheeks. She fought the urge to retch.

It had to be a nightmare. Soon she'd wake up to find everything normal. She would be in some motel along the way, thinking about sidetracking to yet another out-of-the-way museum or shopping mall. Her head would be clear. She would be able to think logically.

She glanced quickly around the room again, hoping against hope that something in her brain would click and make sense of it all. But it didn't. Everything still remained fuzzy, out of sync. She felt like someone trapped in a time warp, unable to move forward or backward, caught up in a nightmare of disorientation. From nowhere flashes of unfamiliar faces and sounds invaded her mind's eye. Everyone wore white and hurried here and there. No one smiled.

Lost in her world of disjointed images, Leza didn't hear the light tapping at the door. A tall, jeans-clad man entered the room, and Leza flew to her feet and flattened her body against the wall.

"Keep away from me!" Her breath came in jagged spurts.

"Easy, I'm not going to hurt you, Leza." His only movement was the nonthreatening gesture of raising both hands outward, palms toward her.

"Who are you? What do you want? Where am I?" Leza hurled the string of questions at him, her voice rising to a frenzied pitch as she inched herself into the corner between the wall and the dresser. It didn't register that he had called her by name.

"My name is Jared Sentell. This is my home," he answered, his voice calm and even. "I figured the phone disturbed you and thought I'd see if you needed anything." He eased back into the open doorway. "I'm going back downstairs. Lock the door behind me. Call your family, or a friend. Tell them you're at Summerset. Anyone in town can tell them how to get here. Call the sheriff if you want. He'll vouch for me. The number's in the book in the drawer." He reached for the doorknob. "Then come on downstairs. You have to be starving. You haven't eaten in more than eighteen hours. There's a robe in the closet." With that, he closed the door and his footsteps faded down the stairs.

Leza wasted no time in scurrying across the room to lock the door. Ignoring the pain in her limbs, she fairly flew to the phone and dialed her parents' number. Only when the recording reminded her that she must first dial one and then the area code did she remember she had been away from home for days. She sank to the bed.

What now? Home and help were over four-hundred

miles away. Steven. Yes, she could call her brother. He would help, just like always.

Quickly she dialed his number. Her fingers fumbling with the mechanics of dialing until she was forced to hang up and start over. At last it began to ring. Instead of feeling reassured, her stomach knotted when she heard Steven's familiar "Hello, Colletti here."

Leza tried to speak, but the words wouldn't come.

"Is anyone there?" Steven sounded irritated.

She slammed the receiver into the cradle and yanked her hand back as if the phone had become a vile, wretched thing. Just what, her new-found independence demanded, was she doing? She couldn't keep running to Daddy and Big Brother all her life. She couldn't think straight, she really felt as if she'd been drugged.

Besides, what could she tell Steven? That she'd just awakened in a stranger's bed, wearing nothing but an oversized T-shirt? That her body was a mass of bruises and scratches, suggesting—only suggesting because she had absolutely no recollection—that something horrible had happened to her? And how long had she been here? She had no idea, but the man named—oh, God, she'd forgotten his name already—had just told her she hadn't eaten in eighteen hours. Had she been with him all that time? And how had she met him?

Leza stood abruptly and steadied her legs against the bed. Her head ached and she felt dizzy and weak. She had to pull herself together, try to figure out what all this meant and what she must do.

Restlessly pacing the length of the room once, then twice, Leza's mind reeled with indecision. She suddenly felt warm and out of breath. She had to have fresh air. Skirting the antique desk, she opened the French doors and welcomed the spring air that caressed her skin. Looking out, she saw what was obviously a well-run ranch, a ranch of some proportion if the size of the barn and other outbuildings were any indication.

She glanced back into the bedroom, seeing it this time with the unerring eye for detail that made her excel in her work. Surely a man bent on no good wouldn't bring his victim to his home, volunteer his name, and then tell her to call the sheriff. But what was his connection with her? Did she dare trust him? Did she have a choice? Even if she had no memory of the past eighteen hours, something terrible had obviously happened.

She needed answers. And if that meant going downstairs and confronting her nameless host, then that was exactly what she would have to do.

THREE

Huge and airy, the country kitchen was every woman's dream with its refreshing blend of nostalgic charm and modern efficiency. An enormous oak table, flanked on both sides by long, sturdy benches and on each end by captain's chairs, stood at the far end of the room before a cozy bay window which, like every window in the room, was draped with curtains of blue-and-white gingham. All in all, it was a room made for a family, a family with many children, all laughing and teasing and loving. A small calico kitten dozed contentedly on a braided rug, completing the homey picture Leza had conjured up in her mind.

Her host stood at an island range, diligently chopping onions, peppers, and mushrooms. Leza hadn't made a sound when she entered the kitchen, but he seemed to sense her presence and glanced her way.

"I see you found something to wear." His observation, although casual enough, put Leza on guard. The robe, several sizes too large for her, hung loosely from her shoulders and dragged along the floor with each

33

movement. "Come on in and have a seat," he invited with a one-handed gesture, indicating that she was to sit at the breakfast bar to his right. "How do you feel?" he asked when she hesitated in the doorway.

"Physically, I *feel* every muscle in my body." She wasn't certain if she liked the way his cool gray gaze studied her. She tugged the robe tighter around her body. The bulky garment made her feel like a child playing dress up, and she didn't like the feeling. Suddenly a weakness spread through her, giving her no time to dwell on her insecurities. He was at her side immediately, lending support when her knees buckled.

She must have gone pale because he asked, "Are you going to be sick?"

"No, I'll be okay in a few minutes," Leza answered shakily, grateful for his arm as he ushered her to the bar stool. His size was intimidating, almost suffocating. Something told her he sensed her discomfort, and she was relieved that he sat down before she did. Despite her uneasiness, she found herself studying him more closely than was polite.

His features were dark and lean, suntanned to a coppery brown. His nose was straight, only slightly flaring at his nostrils; his cheek bones high, his jaw and chin juttingly firm. All in all it was a handsome face, a face saved from harshness by the warmth in his soft gray eyes and the gentle curve of his mouth. She saw gentleness and strength; she saw compassion and ruthlessness. But more than these things, she saw concern— and something else, something so intense that it made her look away. How was it possible, she asked herself, to read so much in the visage of a stranger?

"Really, I'll be all right. I'm just weaker than I thought," Leza reassured him, instantly wondering why she found it necessary. She was obviously the one in distress. "Please, won't you tell me what's happened?"

He studied her for a moment, seeming to weigh her request before he stood and returned to the range.

"Later," he said. "You need to eat first." He quieted her with a frown. "Right now, I'm hungry enough to eat . . . ," he scrunched up his nose in comical disdain, ". . . a pizza, and I hate pizza."

Leza couldn't help smiling. "That's un-American," she quipped, part of her only too ready to delay finding out what had happened. The tension flowed from her while she watched him whip the eggs into a frothy mixture. "You certainly look like you know what you're doing." The smile he flashed at her was as genuine and unexpected as the rush of warmth it created in her.

"The Galloping Gourmet I'm not, but I put together a mean omelet. Cheese?" He held up a bowl of grated American for her approval. "Coffee?" he offered when she said yes to the cheese.

"Yes, please. I need something to shake the fog I seem to be in this morning." Declining sugar and cream, Leza sipped at the fragrant brew while he poured the fluffy concoction of eggs into a hot cast-iron skillet.

"It's probably the aftereffect of the sedative they gave you at the hospital. And it's not morning," he added, effectively blocking any questions. "We're about to have supper."

His offhanded reference to a sedative explained her inability to think, to remember.

"You mean it's six o'clock in the evening? What happened to . . ."

"After you've eaten," he said and placed a plate before her.

"But . . ."

"Eat," he bullied gently, then took his own plate to the opposite end of the bar.

Still too weak to argue, Leza watched him slice off one end of his omelet and place it in his mouth. The aroma of cheese and onions and peppers reminded her that she was starving. Although he'd told her upstairs how long it had been since she'd eaten, she couldn't remember. That persistent blank spot in her memory was doing more than confounding her; it was beginning to make her angry. But the anger didn't outweigh the hunger, and Leza devoured her meal while her coffee grew cold.

"That's encouraging." He warmed her cup with fresh coffee. "You must be feeling better."

Leza's anger seemed to dissipate with her hunger. "Do you realize I don't know anything about you, except that you put together a mean omelet and hate pizza? I've even forgotten your name." The old-fashioned wall phone beside her rang demandingly, startling Leza with its unexpected shrillness. Casually pushing his stool back, he rounded the end of the bar to quiet the offending instrument.

"Jared Sentell," he answered on the second ring, neatly reintroducing himself to Leza at the same time. "Yes, Lis. . . . No, I haven't heard from Mack. Is there a problem?" He braced one hip against the counter and listened attentively while the person he'd called Lis carried on the burden of the conversation.

It wasn't in Leza's nature to eavesdrop, not even unintentionally, so she mustered the energy to begin clearing away their dishes. Still, it was impossible to keep from hearing his end of the conversation.

"No, I missed him last night." He shifted positions, placing his back to Leza. "I had to leave before he got here. There was some . . . trouble I had to tend to."

Another silence filled the cozy kitchen, prompting Leza to look up from scraping the leftovers into the garbage disposal. His demeanor was serious now, his irritation evident by the way he threaded his fingers through the thickness of his raven hair.

"Yes, of course you were right to be concerned. Mack should have called me himself. Make my airline and hotel reservations and I'll see you early tomorrow." Almost as an afterthought he added, "Cancel all my . . ." He chuckled then and Leza imagined the smile that must have spread across his face. "Good girl . . . and don't worry so, Lis, I'll take care of everything."

His words, the way he said them made Leza jerk her head up. She stared at the broad expanse of Jared's back. Those last few words triggered a memory. *I won't leave you, angel. I'll take care of everything.*

Bits and pieces of the scene at the hospital played out in her mind, racing in and out of each other in a confusing and frightening game of tag. Mental images formed, swirling and fading—Jared following her down the long corridor and brushing past a stunned orderly to sit defiantly beside her, a puddle of water between mud-caked boots. And then the questions—so many personal questions.

She closed her eyes tightly against the memories and groped for the counter for support as she recalled her violent protests at being admitted to the hospital, the same hospital where Steven worked. Try as she might, she couldn't shut out her incoherent pleading with Jared not to leave her. What had made her trust this perfect stranger so totally when she should have been terrified by any man?

Her head began to pound with the realization of what she had done. Although she had no memory of the assault the doctor had suggested, Leza knew she couldn't have faced Steven's pity again. Thank God her driver's license was still in her married name. Surely no one would associate Leza St. Clair with Steven Colletti. Chances were good that he'd never even know she'd been at the Medical Center.

"Are you all right?"

Startled by his voice, Leza jerked her head up to see Jared coming toward her. Gratefully, she accepted his help as he led her to the table. "I . . . I seem to remember . . . the emergency room," she stammered, sinking into the captain's chair he pulled out for her. Jared straddled the bench to face her.

"Anything else?" He leaned forward and braced both forearms on his thighs.

"No."

"The doctor said it might come back like that—in fragments. Just take your time and try not to be upset by it."

"Try not to be upset!" Leza suddenly screamed at him, her closely bridled composure slipping now. "That's easy for you to say. Your memory's not full of holes. Your body hasn't been violated!" She saw the control it took for him to keep from reaching out to her. The thought of being touched was terrifying. She jumped to her feet and spun around to put the dining table between them. "And just how do I know you're not the monster who—" For a fleeting moment he looked as if she'd slapped him with her unjust accusation, but then he spoke so softly she had to strain to hear him.

"We both know that isn't the case, Leza."

Tension hung in the fading light of day as they faced each other, neither knowing exactly what to expect from the other. Then, just as suddenly as it had flared, her temper ebbed, leaving her shaken with the unfairness of her indictment.

"I'm sorry. It's all so hard to take in, especially since I don't remember anything," she apologized, not knowing why she'd been so hostile. He was only trying to help. "You know my name. Have we met before?"

"Not before last night. I checked your purse for your ID," Jared explained. "Tell me everything you can remember."

Anxious to have her burst of anger forgotten and to learn what she could, Leza took her seat. "I'm . . . I'm not sure what I can tell you. There are times I think I recall something, but before it becomes clear it fades away. Everything is rather sketchy." A thoughtful scowl creased her forehead. "Rain? A pickup?"

Jared nodded, reaffirming her impressions. "Let's start from the beginning. You're from Odessa, right? So what are you doing four-hundred miles from home?"

She could have tried to explain how meaningless the last two years had been, her error in judgment in marrying Don, how Amy's death had left a void in her life. But he was a stranger. It was best to stick to generalities.

"To make a long story short," she began, "I have a new job in Rosemont. I left home Monday morning and . . . I don't . . . remember anything after . . . Waco," she stammered on, more to herself than to Jared.

"Waco?"

She glanced up to see the questions on Jared's face. "I didn't take the straight-shot route by way of I-20," she explained. "I'm on vacation and was sightseeing. But where did I go after Waco?" So many unanswered questions rattled around inside her head.

"Just take it easy. It'll all come back to you in time."

It was then that the absolute helplessness of her situation struck her. She stood and walked to the back door. Crickets were chirruping. The air was sweet with the scent of freshly cut grass. A dirt dauber buzzed harmlessly around its nest of red clay in one corner of the porch. All was well with the world—and yet, here she was in a beautiful old house with a stranger who probably knew more about what had happened to her than she did because right now she was unable to recall the past or comprehend the future.

She turned to face the room and the man who had

done so much to help her. Somehow, between Odessa and Rosemont, she'd lost control over her life. Now she had to get it back.

"Thank you for your help, Mr. Sentell, but I can't continue to be a burden to you." Leza walked back into the room, rubbing the stiffness in her neck that was threatening to turn into a headache. "You obviously have troubles of your own and I'm only adding to them. If you'll tell me where I can find my clothes, I'll be on my way."

"And where will you go?" he asked, pointedly ignoring her question. "I don't think you're ready to manage on your own."

Unintentionally his words rekindled her anger. What right did he have to make such a presumption? She had a mind of her own; she could take care of herself.

A plan began to formulate. Steven wasn't expecting her at any particular time. This had been one of the things they'd agreed on before she'd left home: She'd call and check-in from time to time so no one would worry, but she would arrive when she arrived. She could make up a story, explain her delay somehow, then find a place to regain her strength and composure before facing him. It wasn't the best of plans, but it was all she could manage under Jared's cool, self-assured gaze.

"I'll get by," Leza said stubbornly, straightening to her full height of five-six. "Now, where are my things?"

"There wasn't much left of them. I threw them out." His voice was flat, cold, without a trace of the concern he'd shown before. "And how are you going to be on your way? You have no car, no clothes. There was no money or checkbook in your purse." His words cut through her, reminding her that she was indeed completely alone and helpless.

"I have a car." Leza's jaw jutted out in defiance. "It

stalled on me—in a roadside park . . ." Her words trailed off in bewilderment. "I don't know how I know that, I just do."

"Small red sports car?" At her affirmative nod, Jared stood and guided her back to her place at the table. "We passed it last night on our way into town. Do you remember anything else?"

She shook her head. Every ounce of determination she had just mustered fled with that small bit of recall.

"I have a suggestion," he said after a lengthy pause. "That was my secretary on the phone. I'll be in Houston all week on business. You can stay here and regain your strength before making any decisions."

"I don't know," Leza hedged. "Won't your family mind?"

"There's no one here but me," Jared shot down that excuse neatly. "My housekeeper will be back in the morning, so you won't be alone. And the ranch hands only come to the house for meals, so you won't be disturbed." He sat in the chair opposite her and folded his arms on the table between them. "I think we both know this is the best solution."

Leza was filled with a sudden sense of wonder when she looked across the table. It was as though she had known Jared Sentell forever. Smoke-colored eyes looked back at her and she could well imagine them shimmering with laughter, or smouldering with anger, or even passion. His broad forehead was well-defined by a widow's peak and his thick, dark eyebrows. Straight and proud, his nose flared gently to draw her attention to the provocative swell of his lips. In her brief moment of observation, Leza saw not only the gentleness she already knew he possessed, but his strength and determination. But she also saw more, something less noticeable, something almost overshadowed by the virility of the man. An intense sadness, a loneliness that, for whatever reason, made her equally sad. Someone had hurt him so badly that even in her misery she could see and feel the need in him to love and be loved. Leza knew instinctively that she was seeing a side of him few people, if any, had ever seen.

Giving herself a much needed mental shake, she reined in her thoughts by silently venting her frustration on Jared because, damn him, he was right. Without her car or money, her choices were limited. And then, too, where could she go? Getting in touch with Steven or her parents would put her right back where she'd started. There was no way she could go back to the way things had been. And besides, she thought, with a deep sigh of resignation, she was simply too tired and confused to think of anything else at the moment.

"You're absolutely right, Mr. Sentell. I accept your offer."

Jared hadn't realized that he was holding his breath until he released it in a sigh of relief. He had watched her closely while she weighed her options, and now that she had made her decision he wasn't quite sure how he felt about it.

He leaned back, raising the front legs of his chair off the floor in a nonchalant manner that belied his inner turmoil. To be honest, he was more surprised by his own mixed emotions than by her acquiescence. Even so, he couldn't help wondering just exactly what he had expected. A little more resistance? Perhaps. If her earlier display of willfulness had been an attempt to regain control over a bad situation, why had she given in so easily?

Stop searching for ulterior motives, Sentell, he rebuked himself. Not every woman is devious and self-serving. This one is simply frightened. She needs time to restore herself, time to learn to trust again. His stomach tightened with the painful reminder of his past hurt. Hell, maybe it was time he did the same.

Soundlessly he settled the chair back to its upright position and stretched his right leg to ease the stiffness that had begun to set in.

"Good. I hoped you'd be sensible about this."

"Only to a point," Leza said. "The week you'll be gone should be enough time for me to . . . decide where to go from here."

There it was again, that infernal pang of protectiveness that gnawed at Jared's insides each time she showed signs of vulnerability. He wanted to hold her. "I'll have my foreman take a look at your car," he offered instead.

The telltale droop of her slender shoulders was the signal he had been expecting. "I think you've had just about enough for one day." He stood, and the sound of the chair scraping across the hardwood floor roused the kitten from its nap. It yawned, stretched to its full length, then attacked the first movement it saw—his pants leg. He scooped up the pesky animal and playfully ruffled its fur.

Leza agreed with a weary nod and, smiling, reached out to pet the bundle of energy that was now chewing one of Jared's buttons. "What's her name?"

"I was hoping you could tell me." He hated to see the smile on her lips die. The confused look on her face made him wish he hadn't been so blunt.

"She belongs to me?" She took the kitten and cuddled it to her breast. Jared found that he was fascinated as she patiently stroked the playfulness out of the kitten. The kitten was only a momentary distraction, however, because when Leza looked up there was a willful set to her small chin.

"There are two things I want made clear," she said. "First, I'll pay for my room and board, Mr. Sentell. And second, I won't put you out of your own room any longer."

"Sounds fair to me." Jared was relieved to see the streak of stubborn pride he'd only glimpsed earlier, glad, too, that he hadn't misjudged her after all. She was a fighter. Given time and patience, she would recover. "You can use the room across from mine. The ranch hands are in and out of the house every day for meals," he hurried on to explain when a shadow of wariness crept across her face. "But they won't disturb you on the second floor."

"By the way," he added, his tone growing lighter, "Mr. Sentell was my father and he's been dead almost twenty years. The name's Jared." The smile he flashed her way radiated from his eyes, drawing to life one disconcerting dimple in his right cheek. "I'll check the guest room." With that he left her nursing her coffee and, taking the stairs two at a time, he was there in a matter of seconds. He flipped on the bedside lamp and the room was immediately bathed in a rose-pink glow.

Aside from the obvious—the color scheme and style of furnishings—it was a reverse image of his own room. It was the same size, almost to the inch with the same floor plan—right down to the French doors that connected it to the balcony.

Glancing around, Jared realized that he never actually considered his sister-in-law's influence in decorating his home until he had occasion to come into this room. A confirmed bachelor and a workaholic to boot, he had been perfectly content with hardwood floors dulled from years of neglect and sheet rock walls that always looked as though they could use a coat of paint. A smile tugged at his lips when he recalled not having the heart to say no two years ago to Becky's offer to redecorate. He had made it clear that he would make all the final decisions, but even so, he'd found it difficult to keep her "homey touches" to a minimum. Difficult, yes, but he had managed. Still, when she had asked for free rein with one of the guest rooms, he had given in to her pleas and her soft green eyes, just as Jake was prone to do so often.

It struck him suddenly that something about this room had always bothered him. He couldn't nail it down, even now, but somehow he felt . . . What? That he didn't belong here? Like the proverbial bull in the china shop?

Glancing about the room again, he was acutely aware of an uncomfortable thought that began to form in his mind. Yes, he decided almost instantly, that had to be it. The room was simply too soft, too feminine, too romantic for his taste. Maybe, he realized with a growing sense of unease, he felt uncomfortable here because, with its ruffles and lace and soft pastels, it had come to symbolize the very thing he had vowed never to fall victim to again. And at this very moment, he felt it had been decorated with only one person in mind—Leza St. Clair.

"It's positively beautiful."

Jared turned around to find Leza standing in the doorway. "Too damned frilly to suit me," he grumbled to cover his embarrassment. How could he have let himself be caught like some adolescent, daydreaming about a woman he hardly knew? He didn't like the feeling of vulnerability that washed over him and instantly resented Leza for witnessing that private side of him. It had taken years for him to become an expert at masking his emotions, and he did so now by leaning down and unplugging the telephone beside the bed. Lis would have to confirm his reservations and Leza had enough to worry about without being bothered by a ringing telephone.

"I'm expecting several business calls," he explained. He hesitated in the doorway, some long denied need battling against a stronger, more urgent demand for self-preservation. "Our rooms share the bathroom. Unlock the door when you're finished." Still, he did not leave. "I'm just across the hall if you need anything," he said, turning abruptly and leaving Leza to stare at his departing back.

Perplexed by Jared's brusque behavior, and alone for the first time since waking, Leza could barely keep from racing across the room and locking the door. What a ridiculous thought. She had nothing to fear from Jared Sentell. But the soreness in her body and the blank spot in her memory were brutal reminders that she had something to fear from someone.

Dejected, she sat at the foot of the bed and absently ran her hand over the coverlet of ecru eyelet. Her experienced eye for detail automatically noted the matching canopy and drapes. She stood, and casually wandered about the room, unconsciously appraising first one, then another of the many antiques that complimented the decor.

As feminine as Jared's room was masculine, this one was the epitome of turn-of-the-century charm with muted colors and country French furnishings. The same moss-green carpeting covered the floor, but instead of greens and beiges the scheme was breathtaking with its simple blend of pink and ecru. Smatterings of greenery throughout the room accentuated the verdant hues of leafy vines in the floral wallpaper.

Although her professional expertise centered on visual display, usually in department stores, Leza's reputation for interior decorating was well-known among the elite of the Midland/Odessa area. She knew quality when she saw it, and not one room she'd seen thus far in Jared's house had been decorated with the aid of mail-order catalogs.

Fatigue soon diminished the brief burst of interest Leza had taken in her surroundings. Tightening the sash of the robe, she pulled back the coverlet and climbed wearily into bed.

The minutes dragged by like hours, ticking away slowly with each sweep of the clock's second hand. She was exhausted, and yet rest eluded her.

"Oh, God." Her whisper hung like a cloud of despair in the rosy haze of the room. She hadn't been this troubled since that tragic time so many months ago. Gently rubbing both temples with her fingertips, Leza sat up and took a deep breath. Maybe a long, hot shower would help her unwind.

The bathroom was long and rectangular, and reflected the same country influence of both the upstairs bedrooms. The only thing Leza really noticed, however, was how sadly out of place her handbag, mud-caked and water-stained, looked on the uncluttered counter next to Jared's shaving tree. Remembering his departing words, she locked the door that led to the adjoining bedroom. With a growing sense of guilt, she rested her forehead against the door. She hated being so untrusting. Jared Sentell was an honorable man, a man who wanted nothing more than to help her. So why couldn't she simply accept his help without questioning his motives? This is ridiculous, she told herself while adjusting the water to a temperature just short of scalding. She didn't, however, unlock the door. Instead, she stepped into the shower and proceeded to scrub every inch of her body until it was sore and red. At last the pulsating spray had worked its magic, and she toweled dry, then tugged the T-shirt back on over her damp hair.

Weary, but remembering to unlock the door, she trudged off to bed. But, just as before, could not sleep. So many things kept tumbling through her brain, demanding attention. It was self-defeating to keep going over and over the same ground, so she forced herself not to dwell on her situation. Instead, she thought about

the only comforting thing in her life at the moment—
Jared Sentell.

While she waited for sleep to claim her, questions
about Jared rolled around in her mind. Why had he
stayed with her at the hospital? And what had he been
thinking when he decided to bring her to his home?

Restless, she rolled over and plumped up her pillow.
It took a few minutes, but at last the shower began to
have a soothing effect. She yawned deeply, but perversely continued to pursue her train of thought. The
more she dwelled on it, the less sense it all made. It
was understandable that she hadn't been thinking too
clearly, but what was his excuse? Taking her in could
do nothing but complicate his life.

None of it really mattered, she realized with an even
deeper yawn. He had wanted to help. She had let him.
It was that simple. Another yawn and her eyelids drooped,
then closed.

The dream was pleasant enough at first, in a comic
book sort of way. Everything was brighter than bright
and larger than life. Kindergarten-sized letters labeled
every item in sight: DOOR 12 glowed in bright red;
CHAIR was scrawled in vivid green; an orange arrow
pointed to the light switch where the words LIGHT
SWITCH were stenciled on the WALL and another
arrow, ARROW 2, curled around toward the first one
and identified it, logically enough, as ARROW 1.

What is this place? Leza tried to ask, but the words
got lost in her throat. Her first thought was that she was
back in grade school, but then she realized that in this
dream she was groggy and lying down. Everything was
out of proportion and reminded her of a cartoon—silly
and warped. But then a slender man tagged DOCTOR
leaned over her and peered down through GLASSES
perched upon his nose. He shook his head and clucked

his disapproval. Leza's insides tightened painfully. This isn't funny, she thought, and tried to turn away from his intense scrutiny.

"And where is your nameplate, young woman? Or have you lost it along with your memory?" His tone was laced with disdain, and Leza hung her head in shame. And rightly so. Who with any pride would be caught without her memory?

"I . . . I don't know, DOCTOR." She thought hard. She knew she'd had a memory once, but where had she left it? "Can you help me?"

DOCTOR looked at her with something akin to disgust just as DOOR 12 swung open and a woman in white entered, her SHOES squishing noisily with each step. A four-inch by eight-inch badge hung on a plastic chain around her neck. NURSE was embossed in purple on the yellow badge.

"Here is the chart, but there is no name," she advised DOCTOR.

"You know the procedure, NURSE."

NURSE looked sadly at Leza with huge moppet-like eyes. Then from her pocket, she withdrew a gigantic orange LABEL MARKER and snapped off the letters N-O-B-O-D-Y. Was that a tear Leza saw as NURSE solemnly pinned the word to Leza's hospital gown?

"You have to go now, MISS NOBODY."

"Go? But where? I have no one . . ."

"That's no concern of ours." DOCTOR turned his back. NURSE opened DOOR 12 and faced the opposite WALL.

The hallway outside DOOR 12 receded into a tunneling swirl of color. At the end of the tunnel, a shadowy figure moved toward her.

"Steven," Leza whispered in relief. "Thank God you've come."

"Why did you send for me?" Steven's voice was an unemotional drone, his movements robot-like as he straightened his own nameplate that read NOBODY'S BROTHER.

"Why?" Leza repeated, unable to believe her ears. "You're my brother, Steven. I've been hurt. I need you."

"Hurt, you say?" Steven looked at her, his eyes cold and unfeeling as they slid over her body. Her blood ran cold and his words stabbed through her heart like a dull knife.

"I see what has happened to you. Everyone can see what happened. Your memory is the price you pay for being wicked." She reached for him, and he pulled away. "No! Don't touch me. You are unclean." He turned and began the long walk back through the tunnel of colors.

"Steven," Leza called after him. "Please come back. Don't leave me. I'm frightened. Steven! Steven!" Each word materialized in front of her face, becoming tangible objects as they fell to the FLOOR before her— STEVEN. PLEASE COME BACK. DON'T LEAVE ME. I'M FRIGHTENED. STEVEN! STEVEN! She tripped over the obstacle words that turned red and orange and purple and green, as she struggled to her feet—only to fall again and again. "NO! NO! NO! . . ."

Leza's strangled cries woke her and she sat up with a start. Moonlight filtered through the drapes, casting eerie shadows about the room. She was damp with sweat and trembling with fright. The dreams had plagued her off and on throughout the night, but this one had been the worst. With only one thought in her mind, she dragged herself from the bed and fumbled through the darkness to the bathroom.

Clean . . . must get . . . clean.

Steaming water splattered against her body, across her shoulders, her chest, her back, but she paid no heed to the pain. She turned slowly, allowing the spray to wash away the foulness she feared would always be a part of her. The thought, however vague, worried her. There were no memories to support her fears, so why did she feel this way?

Water . . . not . . . hot . . . enough . . . her befuddled brain insisted, not caring that her skin felt red and blistered beneath the T-shirt plastered to her body.

Only when the near scalding water gradually turned cold did Leza step from the shower, discard the T-shirt in a sopping heap, and stumble back to bed.

Exhausted, she slept, undisturbed and dreamless until dawn. With a somewhat clearer perspective, she sat alone in the early morning hours and carefully planned what to tell Steven. The prospect of lying was disagreeable, but the alternative would mean months of smothering attention. A new life awaited her and all she wanted was to put the past quickly and painlessly behind her.

It was all too clear, now that she thought back. Her first mistake had been agreeing to room with Steven instead of getting her own apartment as she had originally intended. At the time, though, it had seemed like the best way to overcome Mom and Dad's objections to her impending move.

The best way? Who was she kidding? It had just been easier to do it their way than to stand up to them. Now, she realized, that decision had backed her into a corner. Until the swelling and discoloration around her eyes and the slit on her lip healed, there was no way she could face Steven.

Yes, no matter what Jared Sentell's reasons had been, her decision to stay on at Summerset had been the only one that was even remotely practical.

Slipping out of bed and into the oversized robe she'd borrowed the day before, Leza was drawn to the French doors by the sounds of a ranch coming to life outside. The air was fresh and clean after days of rain and she deeply inhaled the rich spring smells of East Texas.

Across the way, hearty masculine voices called to each other, easily drawing Leza's attention with their friendly banter. Young and old alike, the ranch hands were full of vigor as they assembled around the out-buildings, readying for their workday. So caught up was she in the rowdy crew's camaraderie and good-natured jibes that she didn't at first recognize the sense of peacefulness that enveloped her. If ever a place would help heal the spirit, Summerset Ranch was that place.

Naked beneath Jared's robe, Leza wrapped her arms around her middle against the chill of the morning air. Waking up without her T-shirt had been quite a surprise, but inherent good manners had prevented her from rifling through the chest of drawers or the chiffo-robe for something to wear. Later she found the damp T-shirt hanging over the shower curtain rod, and wondered briefly who had hung it there. She hadn't, however, stopped to analyze her obsession with bathing, not even when she recalled dragging herself out of bed during the night to shower in the dark. Still, in the clear light of day, she wondered about the compulsion that had driven her to shower again. But it was enough that she felt clean. Now, if only she didn't feel so helpless.

She suddenly longed for her own things—still packed neatly in her suitcases in the trunk of her car. It would be a small consolation, but surely her own clothing would afford her a small degree of security and help her feel more in control, less of a victim.

Nature chose that moment to intervene when her abdomen cramped painfully. To have no memory of something as devastating as rape was bad enough, but if she had gotten pregnant . . .

Leza shivered, uncertain whether the iciness coursing through her was from the unpleasant thought or from the breeze gently stirring about her. Along with the wind, voices drifted up from below. She leaned forward and, glancing down, saw Jared step off the porch below, a suitcase in one hand, a briefcase in the other.

"Aw, c'mon, Maggie. I'm not going to wither up and blow away in four days just because you're not in Houston to cook for me," he teased the short, round person at his side.

"Don't you git fresh with me, Jared Wade Sentell," Maggie underscored her scolding by the use of his full name. "I may not be your mama, or even kin for that matter, but I've been takin' care of you more'n ten years now and ain't about to stop frettin' at this late date. Now, you go on so I can git back to my work," the woman ordered, this time with a motherly swat across his backside. "And remember to take your vitamins. You've been workin' too hard lately and I ain't gonna have you gittin' rundown and sick on me."

Leza couldn't help smiling when Jared placed a kiss atop Maggie's graying head and said, "What would I do without you?"

"I shudder to think." Maggie's cherub face was aglow as she followed him to the car parked in the rear driveway. Jared tossed his luggage into the open trunk, then looked down at Maggie.

"I don't like leaving now, but the problems in Houston are critical."

"Don't worry, son. I'll take good care of your lady friend," Maggie promised. "You just take care of business and this ol' ranch'll take care of itself."

"Maggie," Jared stretched out her name in mock frustration. "She's not a 'lady friend,' and don't . . ."

"Don't you be a tellin' me to don't, young man."
With that Maggie propelled him toward the open car
door.

From her bird's-eye view, Leza watched Jared slide
behind the wheel. But once the Cadillac started to travel
slowly toward the road, she felt compelled to follow
along the wide veranda that wrapped around the house.
It was illogical, crazy even, but she was suddenly furious that he was leaving. She had known all along that
he was going away. Hadn't he told her so? But he was
really going. Damn him, didn't he know how frightened she was? That he had been her strength through all
of this? She wanted to call out to him to come back, to
take her with him. Instead, through sheer force of will,
she hugged her insecurities to herself and gradually
brought her heart rate back to normal.

Dejected, she made her way back to her bedroom,
but the sound of a car coming up the driveway sent her
flying back to the railing. Her hopes were dashed at the
sight of her own red Corvette in tow behind a black
pickup. Red, as she affectionately referred to the sports
car, looked as pitiful and helpless as Leza felt.

"Mornin', Missy."

Startled, Leza glanced down to see Maggie smiling
up at her.

"You up to eatin' just now?"

Caught completely off guard, Leza could only stammer, "If . . . it's not too much trouble."

"Trouble?" Maggie's laughter brought a tentative
smile to Leza's lips. "Honey, I been up since five
cookin' and feedin' this crew." She glanced toward the
pickup when one of the hands called to her. "You want
anything outta your car?"

"Oh, yes, please," Leza answered with enthusiasm.
"I'll get the keys. My bags are in the trunk."

Maggie stopped her before she could leave. "Jared

gave 'em to John L. first thing this mornin'." She turned back to the men crowded around Red and called, "Bring the Missy's bags to the house." Then to Leza she said, "Your things'll be outside your door. C'mon down after you've freshened up a bit and I'll fill you full of pancakes and sausage."

Leza, glad the older woman had taken charge, nodded like an obedient child. "Would it be all right if I used the phone first?"

"Help yourself." Maggie disappeared into the kitchen.

There was no use putting off the inevitable. The call to Steven would be her first step to setting her life back on track. She knew she'd have to be strong to pull off the string of lies she'd rehearsed during the wee hours of the morning.

The phone was a cold, lifeless thing in her hand, the ringing a flat monotone in her ear. "Mornin', Colletti here."

Leza took a deep breath. "Mornin', yourself, sleepy head." She was amazed at the cheery greeting she managed.

"If it's not my vagabond baby sister. It's about time someone heard from you. Mom's called twice." Steven sounded like the protective older brother Leza had known all her life. "Is anything wrong?" And as perceptive as ever.

"Well," Leza hedged, uncertain she had the mettle to carry through with her plan. "Yes and no." She closed her eyes, as if to gather inner strength. *Forgive me, Steven.*

"All right, Leza, what's the matter? Where are you? Are you okay?"

"Whoa!" Leza, not at all surprised by his reaction, had to force a reassuring giggle. "Not so fast. I'm in San Antonio, and the only fatality is my car." There! The only real lie so far was her whereabouts.

"San Antonio?" Even over the phone, Steven sounded incredulous. "Fatality?"

"If you'll let me explain, I'll save you the trouble of getting worked up over nothing. I've had some car trouble, and you know how hard it is to get parts for that old clunker of—"

"Look, Sis," Steven interrupted, "it'll only take a few hours for me to arrange some time off, then I'll be on my way. Where are you staying?"

"No," Leza said, a little too emphatically. It was typical of Steven to take matters into his own hands where she was concerned. "No, Steven," she repeated, regaining her composure. "The garage has given me a loaner and there's so much to see and do here that I'm actually looking forward to staying for a week or so."

"I know we agreed that you were to have things your own way, but I'm not sure about all this—"

"Don't be such a big brother." It was Leza's turn to interrupt. "I can take care of myself," she forced a reprimand into her gentle scolding. *You haven't done such a good job so far*, her practical side argued silently.

"Old habits die hard. I just can't help worrying about you. You're still not over . . ." Leza could well imagine him standing in his bedroom, shaving cream all over his face as he weighed his choice of words. ". . . everything that's happened."

Damn, how she hated lying to him! "I'll be okay, Steven, honestly." The words all but stuck in her throat. "Would you do me a favor? Call Mom and Dad and explain for me. Dad's not as easily convinced as you are," she teased.

"Sure, but keep in touch."

"I will, and thanks, Steven." She hung up before he could press her for a phone number, and sat for a long moment staring at the phone. How could she have lied so convincingly? And to Steven, of all people, who had never expected anything from her except love. But, reason argued, hadn't she learned from past experience what happened if Steven even suspected that she was unhappy? Or in trouble? Or hurt? Poor Don had learned the hard way when Steven had taken it upon himself to "persuade" him that today's woman needed interests outside her married life. Not long after that Don had agreed, however begrudgingly, to let Leza return to college for the education she had given up to help him with his career.

That, she reminded herself, had been then. This was now. Her new-found resolve propelled her feet to the door where she found her luggage, as promised, sitting in the hallway. It didn't take long to rummage through her things. Then, with makeup bag, her most comfortable jeans and her favorite baggy blouse in hand, she headed for the bathroom.

At first, she avoided the mirror. She wasn't certain she was up to seeing her body completely naked, but after slipping into her bra and panties, she chanced a guarded glance at her reflection. Remembering her reaction the night before, she steeled herself for the sight of the scratches between her thighs and the bruises on her breasts. But the bite mark on her shoulder caused her knees to buckle. The urge to retch was strong and she felt clammy, weak. There was a roaring in her ears, a pounding in her head as she leaned against the wall for support and waited for the shock to wear off. Unexpectedly the door to Jared's bedroom opened and Leza jerked upright at the sound of a startled gasp.

"I'm so sorry, Missy," Maggie apologized. "I . . . knocked," she tried to explain, her eyes downcast as she hurriedly put the stack of towels in her arms into the linen cabinet behind the door. "Don't guess you heard.

Breakfast is hot and waitin'." Not once did she look up while she edged her way out the door.

Too numb to react immediately, Leza was left alone to stare at the closed door. The stricken look on Maggie's face kept flashing through her mind. How could she ever look the woman in the eye again? Or anyone else?

FIVE

The distance from the foot of the staircase to the kitchen could hardly have been more than eight feet, but to Leza it might just as well have been eight miles. She simply could not take the first step that would put her face to face with Maggie.

This is ridiculous, she scolded her image in the hall mirror. It wasn't Maggie's fault that she hadn't answered the knock at the bathroom door. The fact that Maggie had seen her was embarrassing, granted, but she could handle it.

She straightened her shirt, squared her shoulders—and went nowhere. Again, she caught her reflection in the mirror, and it told her the same thing the one upstairs had. She could cover the bruises and scratches on her body with clothes, but it would be a long time before makeup would hide the marks on her face.

"Breakfast is waitin', Missy," Maggie said from the kitchen doorway. Leza forced a smile of acknowledgment, but still couldn't convince her feet to move. Maggie must have sensed her dilemma, because she gently steered Leza toward the table. "You just set down right here."

In no time at all, Leza was enjoying the fluffiest, best tasting pancakes she'd ever eaten. The nicest part of all was that Maggie talked nonstop, her lively prattle about life on Summerset putting Leza more at ease with every minute that passed. It was good sitting there, just listening, not having to respond to Maggie's one-sided conversation. But too soon the interlude was interrupted by the sound of someone stepping onto the back porch. Both women looked toward the screen door to see a sturdily built cowboy step inside and wipe his boots on the mat just inside the door.

Maggie's face came alive with a smile. "Have a seat, John L. I'll have the lunches ready quicker'n you can put two sentences together." They smiled at each other in a comfortable, easy way that made Leza feel as if she were intruding on a special, private joke between two people who had shared everything from laughter to tears over the years. "How about a cup of coffee while you wait?" Maggie asked, filling the cup to the rim before he could answer.

"Sounds good." John L. eased into the spic-and-span kitchen and parked his stocky frame on the breakfast bar stool so that he faced Leza.

Maggie made quick introductions, telling Leza that John L. was Summerset's foreman and her husband of thirty years. It was amazing how efficiently Maggie worked as she talked. She never missed a beat while she wrapped what looked to be over a dozen sandwiches, covered two apple pies with plastic wrap, and filled two one-gallon jugs with iced tea.

"Ma'am," the ranch foreman acknowledged the introduction by tipping his straw hat, then placing it beside him on the breakfast bar. To keep from staring at his hand, for it was badly gnarled, Leza focused her attention on his face.

John L. Barber was a rough looking man, his weathered features those of someone who had seen more than his share of hard work and even harder times. The sweat stains on his hatband told of countless hours in the sweltering East Texas sun. His wiry, salt-and-pepper eyebrows knitted together briefly while his faded blue eyes lingered on Leza's face an instant longer than was polite. There was an uneasy moment when all three realized that he was staring. Embarrassed, he turned his attention to the mug of steaming coffee Maggie had placed before him.

Leza, embarrassed too, dropped her gaze to her near-empty plate. She could understand that he might be taken aback by her unsightly appearance, but it unnerved her to think what might be running through his mind. Thank God Maggie was talking again, even if her voice was a distant buzz inside Leza's head. Was this what she would have to endure from now on: curiosity, speculation, pity?

She knew that she was over-reacting, and quickly decided that it was just plain stupid to let her imagination make her paranoid. But she wasn't imagining the eerie sensation that pulled her away from her thoughts. She glanced up just in time to see John L. look away again. No, it hadn't been her imagination. He was sitting there, watching her, trying to put all the ugly pieces together. She felt dirty. Her throat constricted, almost to the point of cutting off her breath; bile churned in her stomach, making her queasy. She couldn't stand it. Her fingers clenched into tight fists. She just couldn't stand it a minute longer.

". . . later this afternoon."

Leza's head came up again sharply. Had he been talking to her? She glanced first at Maggie, then back to John L.

"I'm sorry. What did you say?"

John L. was standing with his hat back on his head. He heaved a large cooler from the counter and headed for the back door. "Just said I'd check out your car later on today," he said without looking her way.

"Thank you, Mr. Barber."

"Ain't done nothin' yet," he said, carefully keeping his eyes straight ahead. "Later, Maggie." The screen door closed gently behind him.

"He doesn't say much, does he?" Leza said.

"I've known the man some forty odd years, been married to him thirty of 'em, and I'll bet he ain't put more'n three sentences together at once in all that time." Maggie cocked her head to one side, her cornflower-blue eyes widening in mock innocence. "Can't imagine why, now, can you?"

If Maggie was hoping to ease the tension, it worked. "Haven't a clue," Leza said, relieved that she was beginning to feel calm again.

"I can do this, Missy," Maggie said when Leza started to clear away her dishes. "Why don't you take a walk and give Summerset the once-over? The fresh air and sunshine will do you a world of good."

It was tempting, but Leza hesitated. The prospect of encountering any of the ranch hands set her nerves on edge. Almost instantly, her head began to ache. "I think I'll just . . ." What? She couldn't think. Take a nap? She had just gotten out of bed. She began to fidget. ". . . straighten my room and unpack my things, if you're sure I can't help down here." It didn't look as though she had fooled Maggie, but the older woman didn't argue.

Leza suppressed the urge to bound up the stairs. She shut the bedroom door and leaned against it for the few seconds it took to bring her breathing back to normal. The pain in her head promised to blossom into a full-fledged headache and she tried to ease it by gently massaging her temples. She couldn't believe she had reacted so strongly to the simple suggestion that she venture outdoors. Nervously, she paced the length of the room and, as before, found herself on the balcony. What was so threatening out there that she panicked at the suggestion of something as simple as a leisurely walk?

"Damn." She slammed her tightly clenched fist against the railing. If only she knew what she was afraid of . . .

The first thing to come to mind was the possibility that *he* could be out there someplace watching, waiting. The blood coursing through her veins felt like ice water. No! she commanded herself. She had to get control. She was safe in this room, if nowhere else, and she would take her time in dealing with her fears. Life moved slower here. She could go at her own pace. No one would rush her. Hadn't Jared encouraged her to take her time? And hadn't Maggie been more than friendly?

Suddenly, as vividly as if they were in the room with her now, Leza saw Maggie's startled expression and the look of quiet curiosity on John L.'s face. In that instant, it was all too clear: Although she had no memory of the assault, she knew with certainty that anyone looking at her could see what had happened. Wasn't it literally written all over her face?

Instead of making her bed as she had intended, she crawled back into it and pulled the covers tightly over her shoulders. She didn't want to dream again, so she didn't sleep. She didn't want to think, so she stared at the wallpaper, content in the knowledge that she was safe here—safe from prying eyes and pitying glances.

In her state of emotional limbo, she was unaware of the passage of time until Maggie called from the other side of the door.

"Lunch is ready, Missy."

Leza heard, but didn't answer.

"Missy?" Maggie called again, opening the door when there was still no answer.

Leza sat up, but didn't make an attempt to leave the bed. "I'm not hungry, Maggie, but thank you just the same."

Maggie eased into the room and Leza sensed that she understood far more than she let on. "If it's the men, they won't be comin' to the house today. I fixed 'em a lunch and they'll—"

"No. It's not that," Leza lied. "I just don't feel well."

"You just rest up then so you'll feel like comin' down for supper later." Maggie sounded worried, but she didn't press the matter.

"Yes, that sounds fine." Leza tried to be convincing, but was relieved when the door closed and she was alone once again. It wasn't a conscious decision, but somewhere between lunch and supper she realized that she would not be going downstairs again soon.

The days dragged by and Leza literally hibernated in her room. She read all the books and magazines Maggie brought her; she watched game shows and soap operas on the television that had appeared one evening while she was bathing. She felt more and more reclusive with each day that passed, and no amount of coaxing from Maggie could budge her from her room.

Her decision to stay in her room had been unconscious. Her resolve not to dwell on the assault, or the fact that she remembered none of the details, was calculated. The memories would return in time, of that she was certain. She even stopped feeling guilty for lying to Steven. That had been a necessary ploy. But the days of self-imposed isolation began to feed her imagination, exaggerating Maggie's and John L.'s reactions to her battered appearance so much that she couldn't bear the thought of coming face-to-face with anyone. Maggie finally gave up trying to get her to come downstairs and her worried expression became as routine as the meals she served in Leza's room three times each day.

"Come in, Maggie," Leza said on the sixth day to the familiar tapping that signaled mealtime. Maggie entered, empty-handed this time, and went directly to the closet.

"Jared got in late last night," she said over her shoulder. "He wants you to come down for breakfast."

Still in bed, Leza turned her back. "Tell Mr. Sentell I'm not feeling well," she said to the wall.

Maggie dropped a pair of jeans and a powder-blue tank top on the bed on her way out the door. "I'll tell him, but it won't do no good."

Leza wasn't certain what she expected next, but it wasn't having the door to her room pushed roughly open. She sat up with a start to find Jared glaring at her.

"Do you know what time it is?" His tone and rigid stance said clearly that he was annoyed. Dressed in jeans and a western shirt, he was once again the cowboy she'd met her first day here. But something about his manner was different, and Leza braced herself for whatever confrontation he had in mind.

"It's after ten o'clock," he informed her before she could answer. "Maggie tells me you haven't been out of this room since I left. And look at yourself." He gave her a cursory once-over. "When was the last time you combed your hair?" He lifted a limp curl. Leza, reacting purely by reflex, slapped his hand away. His dark eyebrows pulled together briefly, then he picked up her jeans and tank top, and shook them at her. "Or gotten dressed?"

Who was this insensitive clod almost shouting at her?

What had become of the gentle man who had taken her in and responded to her every need with kindness and consideration?

"I . . . I . . ." Lord, how she hated the stammer in her voice. ". . . haven't felt much like getting up," she managed to say, knowing it was a lame excuse, but not knowing how to explain herself.

"Well, you're going out this morning. You're going to get dressed and you're going to come downstairs. After we've eaten, we'll plan our next step."

For a moment Leza was stunned. Then she was angry. "And just how do you plan to make me get dressed and come downstairs?" Wrong move. She flattened her back against the headboard and raised her chin defiantly when he took one menacing step closer. She found her voice just in time. "Brute strength? Strong-arm tactics?"

That stopped him in his tracks.

"You've won this one, angel," he said, the rigid set of his jaw contradicting the calmness in his voice.

He left her then, but she had the distinct and unpleasant impression that he'd left off a very important "But . . ."

Instinct told to her get out of bed and get dressed; stubbornness made her reckless. She should have trusted her woman's intuition because less than five minutes later Jared reappeared, a breakfast tray in his hands. Maggie was hot on his heels with an identical tray of food.

"What do you think you're doing?" Leza couldn't believe that he was actually crawling into bed with her. Maggie placed the tray on Leza's lap and discreetly slipped out the door.

"I asked you a question," Leza said sharply, juggling the tray on her lap and trying to tug the covers over her nightshirt at the same time.

Jared settled his tray across his lap. "I'm about to

have a birthday breakfast," he said, "late though it is, with an ungrateful, slightly bedraggled-looking young woman. Juice?" he offered with infuriating calmness. Leza didn't know what had happened between the time he'd left her room and now, but it was obvious that he'd changed tactics.

"I don't believe this." She tried to inch away, but the tray restricted her movements. "And I won't stand for it!"

She winced at the roguish glimmer in his clear, gray eyes because she suspected that she'd left herself wide open for a teasing. She was right.

"Poor Leza," he said, setting his tray aside. "What can you do? Kick me out of my own house?"

Tears prickled behind her downcast eyes. She was relieved, glad to have this Jared back, and felt that she had let him down somehow by wallowing in self-pity all this time. She hardly noticed when he took her tray and placed it on the floor beside his own.

"I thought you were anxious to be on your way," he said, reaching over to lift her chin and turn her face toward his own. "You're looking much better. The scratches are healing nicely." He turned her head slightly to the side. "And the bruises are fading. Emotionally, however," he said, shaking his head solemnly, "I'd have to say that you're a wreck."

She hadn't cried in all this time; she would not cry now. She would not.

Despite her resolve, her lower lip began to quiver. The tears began to fall. "I just can't put myself on display." She didn't understand it herself, so how could she explain it to him? "Everyone has been so good to me . . ." It was hard to go on; her thoughts were a jumble. "I'm just sick to death of being so damned . . . so damned . . . *pitiful*!" She spit out the last word and leaned into the strong arm that wrapped around her. "I haven't done anything all week except cower like a dog that's been beaten one time too many.'' Angry with herself for being so weak, she wiped away the tears streaming down her cheeks, accepting the napkin Jared offered her. She hated the sniveling tone in her voice, but it felt so good to get it out of her system. "I don't want to go downstairs. I don't want to go outside. I don't want to do anything—'' She tried to stop the tears and sniffled brokenly. "Except . . . shrivel up and die.''

Jared's soft chuckle should have made her angry. Instead, she snuggled deeper into his embrace. "No, Leza,'' he spoke softly against her hair. "We couldn't have that. How would it look on the six o'clock news?'' He pulled back to smile down at her. " 'Pitiful young woman found shriveled up dead in local rancher's bed. Film at ten.' '' She couldn't help laughing, and it felt wonderful.

"That's better,'' he consoled, wiping the tears away with his thumb. "All you need is a change of scenery.'' He stood and pulled Leza to her feet.

"Doing something normal would be a good place to start.'' With that, he propelled her toward the bathroom. When they stood before the mirror, he coaxed her to look at herself. "Do something with your hair.'' He handed her the hairbrush. "Put on a little makeup,'' he suggested, rummaging through her case of feminine paraphernalia. "Paint your toenails—now that's normal— anything that'll bring you back to the land of the living.'' The tiny bottle of Pampered Pink nail polish looked silly in his large, sun-browned hand. She took it from him without looking up.

"I'm not sure I'm ready,'' she confided shakily. "My reactions are so unpredictable. What if someone simply speaks to me and I over-react like . . .''

"Go on,'' Jared said gently. "Like what?''

"It's nothing,'' she insisted. "Really. It's just that

I'm afraid of how I might react—'' She stopped and hung her head. ''—to let's say, one of the men.''

He looked thoughtful for a moment, then turned her to face him. "So that's it," he said as if something had just become crystal clear. "It's going to be okay, Leza. We'll take it one step at a time. Now, get dressed. I'll be waiting for you. Fifteen minutes, not a minute longer, or I'll be back to use those strong-arm tactics you mentioned earlier.''

Downstairs, Jared was angry. Not with Leza, but with himself. Why had he come down so hard on her after learning that she hadn't been out of her room since Monday? Hadn't he spent hours on the telephone learning exactly what to say and do to make things easier for her? He had told the counselor at the Rape Crisis Center in Houston about the partial amnesia and her inability to make decisions. He even mentioned how adamant she'd been about bathing the night he'd brought her to Summerset, and that he had heard the shower twice that second night. The counselor assured him these things were perfectly normal. The amnesia was nature's way of protecting her from memories too painful to remember. The obsession with bathing was her subconscious way of cleansing her body, as well as her psyche. And if Leza was typical, it would probably be several weeks before she was able to settle down to any real decision making.

After numerous sessions of telephone counseling and hours of reading pamphlets the counselor had sent to his hotel, Jared knew that each rape victim had her own way of dealing with the trauma her mind and body had suffered.

Still, knowing all of this, he had over-reacted, treating her like a spoiled child instead of a woman filled with fear and pain. She needed his help. He should have been perceptive enough to realize that something had happened to force her into hiding. After talking briefly with Maggie, he remembered something else the counselor had told him. Many times victims of rape become obsessed with a feeling of uncleanliness. So obsessed, in fact, that they often believe everyone, strangers as well as friends and family, could simply look at them and somehow know every detail of the assault. He had learned so much this past week, and now it was time to put that knowledge to use.

From the corner of his eye, Jared saw something slinking toward him. He waited, then scooped up the kitten just as it attacked his boot. He settled the small animal in his lap and smiled as it gnawed playfully on his hand, distracting him only momentarily.

Slowly his anger at himself abated and he began to form another strategy. Originally, he wanted only to provide Leza with a place to stay and time to pull herself together, but sometime between Monday morning and now he realized that wouldn't be enough. Since she obviously didn't want her family involved, it looked as though he would have to be the one to furnish the moral support she so desperately needed. Oddly enough, he wanted to be the one to help.

Things had gone well in Houston. He had managed to work out all the problems with the Petro-Chem/Sentell Enterprises merger without alienating any of the parties involved. With the crisis behind him, he wouldn't be needed that much at the office. He could, he decided, spend more time at Summerset.

When he had started out some twenty years ago, Summerset hadn't been nearly its present size and the cornerstone of Sentell Enterprises, J & J Swabbing, had been a small outfit all the old-timers thought would never make it. Swabbing, the process of cleaning out oil wells, had been hard and dirty work, a job made harder and dirtier because they'd had two trucks and only the two of them to do a job that usually required two to three men per truck. But luck had been with him and Jake, and together they had turned it into a thriving, prosperous endeavor. So prosperous that Jared spent less and less time at Summerset. That's when John L. and Maggie Barber became a permanent part of his life.

John L. had been a roughneck in the early days of the oil boom around Kilgore, but a floor accident left his right hand mangled, and for years, useless. No one wanted a cripple on the floor. John L., a man with a feisty young wife and three children, was forced to take any menial job he could find. Jared's and John L.'s paths had crossed many times and one night at a favorite watering hole, the two drunken oil field workers— one in his prime, the other on the down slide—came to what would later prove to be the best decision either ever made: John L. would take over Jared's responsibilities at the ranch.

John L. was good at his job as foreman of Summerset, and secure enough in his position that Jared's presence was always welcome. Finding something to do would be no problem, and Jared hoped that a little physical activity would be just what the doctor ordered to take Leza's mind off her troubles.

The kitten nestled in his lap came to attention when Leza stepped into the kitchen. Jumping to the floor, it wound itself around her ankles, then sprinted for the back door where a green lizard skittered on the outside of the screen.

This was the first time Jared had seen her in anything other than rags or one of his T-shirts or that silly nightshirt she'd been wearing earlier. He could tell by the way she moved that the soreness was gone, but her skin was still somewhat discolored and sallow. Still, he liked what he saw. A pastel print blouse, open and knotted at the waist, covered the pale-blue tank top he'd seen on her bed. Her jeans fit snugly from hip to ankle and the sneakers on her feet were so clean that they had to be brand new. The only makeup he detected was a little blush and some mascara. Her hair, as black as his own, had been brushed to a glossy sheen and fell around her face in soft, loose curls.

"Thirteen minutes, thirty-three seconds," he said, guessing at the elapsed time while glancing at his watch. When he looked up, he let his gaze slide again from her head to her toes. "Not bad, not bad at all." He loved the way she blushed at the double meaning of his compliment. "If you're ready, we'll take Hoover with us. She could use some fresh air and sunshine, too."

"Hoover?"

"Yeah. Since you didn't remember owning a cat, I figured it probably didn't have a name, so I took the liberty."

"But why Hoover?"

Holding up one hand as if to say "Wait one," he pinched off a piece of raw ground beef that Maggie had shaped into a meatloaf. Casually resting one hip against the counter, he dropped the meat on the floor. Hoover, moving like a streak of lightning, abandoned the lizard to pounce upon the tiny morsel, inhaling it with such speed that Leza could only blink in amazement.

Jared looked deadpan from Hoover to Leza. "And you never have to change bags."

By the time lunch had come and gone, Leza had helped paint the back steps, mix feed for the stock, and change a tire on the tractor. She doubted that she'd been of any real help, but Jared praised her efforts, teasingly proclaiming that he was putting her on the payroll. Now that the hottest part of the day had started to redden her fair skin, he insisted that she and Hoover rest in the shade while he finished mending a small section of fence.

She paid little attention to his chore at first, but as time wore on and she lost interest in the landscape and in Hoover's misbehavings, she found her gaze wandering time and time again to where he worked. He was shirtless now, and his sun-kissed skin glistened with perspiration.

He had just replaced the top two railings when she saw him kneel down to inspect the corner post. He smiled, and Leza's heartbeat accelerated when that one tiny dimple in his right cheek sprang to life. She had no time to examine her reaction because he reached out, tentatively it seemed, then withdrew his hand without touching what had caught his eye. He studied the situation for a moment, then tugged his work gloves from the hip pocket of his Levi's and pulled them on. Then, carefully, he began to work the delicate structure of straw, grass, and string from its resting place in the joint of the lowest railing.

Leza, reclining against the trunk of a large red oak, sat up on her knees for a better look. Nestled safely in the small nest were two tiny speckled eggs. Ever so gently, Jared placed the nest on the ground, then went back to work. Half an hour later, he straightened and, placing both hands on his hips, stretched backward to ease the stiffness in his back and shoulders. Then, with the same tenderness as before, he picked up the nest and settled it precisely where he had found it.

Seeming to feel her gaze upon him, he glanced Leza's way, and she smiled. Taking a blue bandana from his other hip pocket, he smiled back and wiped the sweat from his face and neck. He started toward her, and Leza was struck by the natural grace in his stride.

She had noticed before that he was an exceptional looking man. There was no way to miss it. But without his shirt and with his jeans riding low around his waist, it was difficult, if not impossible, not to notice every detail of his powerfully built body. Tall and lean, he epitomized everything masculine. His chest was broad, covered with a curly mat of dark hair that tapered down his abdomen to disappear into the waistband of his jeans. His arms were long and muscular, the biceps large and well-defined. His hands, the same hands that had handled the nest so tenderly, were strong, with long tapered fingers that looked as though they could easily bend nails.

Was this a good sign, she wondered, that she still held a healthy appreciation for masculine beauty? She hoped so, realizing that she hadn't thought about her predicament all afternoon.

With that realization, hope was born. Maybe it had all been a mistake. Maybe she hadn't been raped. What if she had just had car trouble and something else had happened to her while she was trying to get help? Hadn't it been dark? Couldn't she have been sideswiped by a passing car, or lost her footing on a hillside and fallen? Elation filled her and she wanted to weep with relief. Then she remembered the hospital, the fingerprints on her breasts, the bite mark on her shoulder, and she felt ill. Her stomach knotted painfully. There was no way she could explain away those facts.

"Man, that big old bed's sure gonna feel good tonight," Jared said, pulling her from her disturbing thoughts as he stretched out to lay on his back in the grass beside her. Leza was relieved to see that he was wearing his shirt, although he hadn't taken the time to button it. She poured a cup of cold water from the thermos, handed it to him, and scooted back to her position against the tree. He sipped at the water, then poured some on the bandana and laid it across his bare chest to cool himself. Taking a deep breath, he just lay there, staring at the clear blue sky overhead.

The silence they shared was in no way awkward. To the contrary, it was relaxed and comforting. It had been like this all day. What conversation there was centered on their chores, Hoover, and the ranch. As Leza watched the steady rise and fall of his chest, she couldn't help wondering what was going through his mind.

Almost as if he heard her thoughts he said, "Running Sentell Enterprises is challenging as hell, but I forget sometimes how much I love it here at Summerset."

"Your business keeps you away a lot?" she asked, and he merely nodded in response. "If you'd rather be here, why not just walk away from the rat race?"

He didn't answer right away, and when he did Leza could have cried for the sadness in his voice.

"I made a promise a long time ago—" he cut himself short and Leza sensed that he realized he was about to reveal too much. "It's a very long, very boring story and there are much more interesting things for two people to talk about on a day like this." He rolled over onto his stomach and looked up at her. "Not a bad start," he said.

She knew that he was uncomfortable talking about himself and changed the subject back to her. "No, not a bad start at all." Before she knew it, he pulled up to tweak her sun-reddened nose.

"We'll have to see about getting you a hat."

For a moment, Leza thought he might be thinking about kissing her. As illogical as it was, considering her circumstances, she wanted him to kiss her, wanted him to hold her. Yes, Jared's arms would make everything all right again.

But he didn't. His eyes trained on something in the distance. It took a few seconds, but soon she saw what had captured his attention.

The sparrow winging toward them circled once, then twice, then lit on the corner post. Both she and Jared sat perfectly still, scarcely breathing. Would the mother detect that the nest had been tampered with? If so, would she settle in or desert the unhatched nestlings?

Leza heard a quiet, muttered curse beside her when the bird chirruped, then flew away. In a matter of seconds, it returned, and after much flittering and prancing, it finally settled on the nest.

A smile crossed Jared's handsome features. "Let's go home," he said happily, taking Leza by the hand and heading for the house.

SIX

During the days that followed, they slipped into a comfortable routine. Each morning Jared called for Leza to "Come and get it," on his way past her door, and gradually she began to look forward to the beginning of each new day.

Breakfast was their quiet time—time spent with nothing more conversational than outlining their plans for the rest of the day or discussing the headlines of the *Rosemont News*.

Things became so routine that Leza didn't notice when Jared started leaving for the office later each morning, or when he started coming home earlier each afternoon. She did notice, however, that while he was away she became restless and moody. There was, after all, only so much to do after making her bed and straightening her room. Thankfully, Maggie recognized the problem, and by mid-week Leza was occupied with all kinds of housework. She vacuumed. She dusted. She helped plan and prepare the noon and evening meals.

Being busy helped, but even Leza saw it for what it

was—therapy, pure and simple, a healthy diversion that kept her from brooding over her precarious circumstances. Therapy that worked—most of the time. Only when one of the ranch hands came to the house would she quietly disappear, not to be seen again until Jared walked in the door.

Healthy diversion or not, housekeeping chores soon became as monotonous as doing nothing, and toward the end of the week she gladly accepted Maggie's invitation to make the twelve-mile trip into Rosemont for the weekly grocery shopping. Leaving the relative safety of Jared's home was a scary proposition, but Leza knew that it was time to test her reactions to life outside of Summerset.

Technically, Leza noted right away, Rosemont was too large to be considered a town and too small to pass as a city, but the thriving community fairly bustled with activity.

"Ain't it somethin', Missy?" Maggie said, beaming with pride while she drove through what she called "Old Town." "My granddaddy and daddy helped lay these brick streets back when Rosemont was just buddin' out." They exchanged grimaces at the unintentional pun. "Up till 'round the 1930s the town was hardly more'n a muddy spot in the middle of nowhere, but old man Grissom's gusher changed all that. Oil derricks sprung up ever'where; in pastures, in vacant lots, and in backyards." She laughed softly, remembering. "Even the old churchyard wasn't spared." Maggie's enthusiasm was contagious and Leza became intrigued by her reminiscing.

"I'll bet it was a sight to see," she said, wanting to hear more.

Maggie nodded, pausing just long enough to wave to an old couple on the sidewalk. "Oh, yes, indeed it was. I was just a little girl, mind you, but I remember most of it. The town started growing by leaps and bounds. Only Kilgore's fields and Spindletop down in Beaumont was bigger'n ours, and before anybody was really ready for it, lots of folks in these parts was filthy rich. Even men who'd never made more'n a dollar a day was bringin' home more money'n they'd ever dreamed possible.''

''Did Jared get his start here?'' Leza asked. She hadn't been so wrapped up in her own problems that she hadn't wondered about Jared's past.

''It was a mite later, of course, but when you're raised in the oil patch it tends to get in your blood. Him and Jake roughnecked with John L. some in those early years.'' She glanced at Leza, and the pride she'd shown in her hometown was nothing compared to the expression on her face now. ''My John L. was a motor man back then, before his hand got all mangled.'' Some of the sparkle dimmed in her soft blue eyes. ''But that's another story,'' she said, seeming to shake off memories she kept carefully tucked away. ''Anyway, one day them two boys just happened to be at the right place at the right time, and found themselves the proud new owners of a small swabbing outfit. Course, they didn't know it at the time, but the blamed thing was 'bout to go under.'' She laughed then. ''But I guess you could say ignorance is bliss. All them two 'worms'—that's what they call greenhorns in the oil patch—wanted was a chance, and they took it and turned that worthless outfit into what was the beginning of Sentell Enterprises.''

''Sounds like the Sentell brothers had a lot going for them,'' Leza prompted when Maggie became suddenly quiet, thoughtful.

''Well, yes and no. Their old man wasn't much help. Then there was Vietnam . . .''

Leza got the impression that Maggie had touched on something she was uncomfortable getting into, and although Leza was curious, she respected the older woman's reticence. "Rosemont doesn't look much like an oil town these days. What happened?"

"Same thing that happened all over Texas," Maggie began. "The bottom dropped out of the oil business. Quicker'n you could say dry hole, people who'd been ridin' high and mighty lost it all. Jared and Jake were lucky. They hadn't tied all their money up in oil. Jared had de-versy-fied their assets—that's the fancy phrase he uses—dabbled their money into first one thing, then another; bricks, lignite coal, and other stuff I don't know too much about. Sentell Enterprises did all right." Maggie's face fairly glowed as she talked about Jared's and Jake's success.

"I love happy endings," Leza said, if a bit wistfully.

"Yeah, me too, but that ain't all. It was clear that the good people of Rosemont had to do somethin' to save the town. It was right under our noses from the very start." Leza should have known there was more to the story, and continued to be a good listener while Maggie went on with her tale. "Roses! Our good, rich soil and our climate were perfect for growin' roses. Wasn't long before Rosemont was plantin' and shippin' roses all over the states." Again, she seemed to swell with pride. "Now just look at us. We're right back where we started. Maybe even better off than before 'cause we still got the oil fields, if and when oil prices get better, and we've got our roses. Each October we have our Rose Cavalcade, complete with fancy balls, a parade, and a real, live, honest-to-goodness coronation. The Historical Society's been sprucin' up the Old Town District. Even got Jared involved this year when he bought the old Prescott place." She turned then to grace Leza with one of her endearing smiles. "It's called the Dixieland Hotel now, and was the most famous bawdyhouse in these parts during those oil boom days."

She stopped at a red light. "We even ——
fancy shoppin' malls on the other side o——
said, getting back to Rosemont's presen——
like to see it?"

"Not today, Maggie," Leza said, but —— ——
thanks. "Maybe tomorrow, if it's okay w—— you."
Although she was tempted to take a quick look at where
she'd be working in a few short weeks, she couldn't
take the chance of running into Steven—not even a
remote chance.

"Hey, I'm easy," Maggie said cheerfully, and turned
her attention back to driving.

Leza was no stranger to the oil fields of Texas. She'd
grown up in Odessa, where the oil industry was the
economic foundation of the area. All of Texas had
suffered because of the oil slump, and Leza admired
this small East Texas town for its tenacity, for its will to
survive.

She loved her native West Texas, where the air was
fresh and arid but flowers and grass and trees were in
short supply. The contrasts between its wide-open spaces
and Rosemont's rolling countryside were so great that
she couldn't help making comparisons. Although both
were beautiful, in different ways, it didn't take long for
Leza to fall in love with Rosemont's tree-lined streets
and neatly manicured lawns. Civic pride was evident
everywhere, especially in the way homes and businesses were landscaped, many with brightly colored
azaleas and roses and flowering dogwoods. She had
become so engrossed with the town's storybook perfection that Maggie's voice was an unwelcome intrusion.

"Well, here we are," she announced, parking the
station wagon in front of McElvey's Grocery.

Addison and Julie McElvey greeted them at the door,
welcoming their longtime customer and her companion
with genuine affection. At first Leza was uncomfort-

, but when no one paid undue attention to her, or
topped to stare when they passed in the aisles, she
slowly began to warm to the small-town friendliness.
It was wonderful to be free of the paranoia that had
become a constant part of her for so long. Paranoia?
The thought surprised her. Had it been that bad? Yes,
she had to admit, paranoid was the only word to describe how she had been feeling. Maybe she was just
getting better, she thought, happily taking her part of
the marketing list and making her way toward the pro-
duce department.

By noon, they were headed back to the ranch. She'd
laughed and talked freely all morning long and it seemed
to her that it had been a long time since she'd felt this
good. Before she knew it, they were turning onto the
red clay road that wound its way from the main road to
the farmhouse she was fast beginning to think of as home.

Jared's black pickup was parked in the grass behind
the house. A hose and a bucket filled with sudsy water
were close at hand, and Leza's heart skipped a beat
when Jared appeared on the back steps. Clad only in
cut-off jeans, he looked nothing like the high-powered
executive she'd sent off to the office only three hours
earlier.

"Just in time," he greeted them, taking a bag of
groceries from Leza. "I'll help Maggie with these if
you want to change and lend a hand with the truck."

He smiled down at her then, and it crossed Leza's
mind that he could charm the spots off a leopard with
that wonderful, one-dimpled smile. Quickly pushing
aside the wayward thought, she decided that washing
the pickup was as good a way as any to pass the time
before lunch. In less than five minutes, she'd changed
into her most comfortable faded jeans, opting for a
loose fitting sweatshirt instead of the tank top she usually favored.

"Hey," she called to get Jared's attention. "You missed a spot." Using the hose to point at the whitewall he was scrubbing, she barely missed him with the volley of water.

"Careful," he warned, falling backward to avoid being doused. "That's how wars are started." He cocked one dark eyebrow at her and reached for the hose.

"Oh, no, you don't." Leza sidestepped him nimbly, dragging the hose with her to put the pickup between them.

Feigning a look of innocence, Jared followed her around the front of the truck. "C'mon, Leza, if I don't rinse the soap off before it dries, it'll streak and I'll have to rewash the whole thing." The words were sincere, but the glimmer in his eyes warned her not to relinquish her claim on the hose. He stopped when she laughed and continued to back away. "Do I look like the type of man who would—"

Breaking off his words, he dashed toward her, grabbing for her and the hose at the same time. He would have had her, too, if he hadn't stumbled over the bucket of wash water. Leza reacted by lunging to one side. He missed her by inches, and went sprawling into the soggy San Augustine grass. The temptation was just too great. Before there was time to consider the consequences, Leza hosed him down good and proper, squealing with a mixture of delight and excitement as they grappled for control of the hose.

Just as he had wrestled it from her hands and was about to turn it on her, Maggie's voice stopped him cold. "Jared Wade Sentell! Quit pickin' on that poor child!"

Jared looked incredulous. Leza had the decency to look chagrined. "Poor child?" he said. "Open your eyes, Maggie, and see who's picking on whom."

Maggie's expression said she wasn't buying what he

was selling. "I don't want to hear it," she said, holding up one hand to silence him. "Just take these towels and finish up." Without another word, she left the damp pair to stare at each other.

"Well, I guess that settles that," Jared said, shaking the water from his dark hair before raking it back into place with his fingers.

"Yep, that settles that," Leza agreed matter-of-factly, but her attention strayed to the water glistening on Jared's bare skin. Fascinated, she let her gaze wander across the breadth of his shoulders when he bent over to towel dry his legs. The play of muscles across his back captured her attention and she had a sudden impulse to reach out and touch him. What would he feel like, she wondered, stifling the urge, and would the muscles in his arms feel as hard as they looked? He straightened then, mopping the towel up and down each arm. Water trickled through the crisply curling hair that covered the expanse of his sun-browned chest. She was unaware that he had stopped drying himself until she looked up to see him watching her watching him.

"I'll clean the inside while you dry it," she volunteered, wanting to kick herself when she felt her face flush. "Where do you keep the vacuum?"

"Try the utility room just off the kitchen." Was she imagining the note of amusement she heard in his voice, she wondered, not daring to turn and look as she bounded up the steps.

The vacuum was exactly where Jared had told her it would be. She picked up the canister and draped the hose around her neck, then grabbed the attachments in her free hand. She felt like a one-man band juggling the canister, the hose and attachments, and sidestepping the dangling cord, but she finally managed to reach the porch.

Jared stood in the pickup's cargo bed, wiping the cab

with a towel. He looked up when Leza appeared at the door and smiled at the predicament she'd gotten herself into. "Looks like you could use an extra pair of hands," he called and threw one long leg over the side of the truck bed.

Hey, lady, what's the matter? You look like you could use a man about now. The words crashed into her brain. Images followed, images so clear and unexpected that she fell against the door. Her head reeled: A young man, stocky and blond, staggered toward her—she saw it plainly. One moment he was standing in the back of a pickup, a red pickup, and the next he was trying to right himself when he stumbled and almost fell over the tailgate. It was all too vivid and then it was gone. She felt the blood drain from her face as she watched Jared's lean frame hit the ground and start toward her.

"You remembered something?" he asked, taking the vacuum from her. "Come sit down." Like a small child, she allowed herself to be led to the wicker settee on the porch. "Tell me," he coaxed gently, taking a seat beside her.

"I . . . I don't know," she stammered, clearly confused. "Everything was so clear for a split second . . . But I don't know exactly what it was."

"Slow down, angel. Just take your time."

The calmness in his voice soothed her and she found the words at last. "Your words, the way you stepped out of the truck, struck a chord in my mind. It happened so quickly and now it's gone." Unconsciously she'd been wringing her hands, and they had turned white from the strain. "Is this how it's going to be until I remember it all?" she asked, biting back the tears she refused to let fall. "Just bits and pieces out of the past to torment me?"

Jared took her hands in his own and gently massaged the warmth back into them. "Things are happening just like the doctor said they would. It's going to take time, but you're strong enough to handle whatever comes your way."

"But I'm scared, Jared. I don't want to handle whatever comes my way." She leaned into him for support. His arms were comforting, strong without being threatening. If she could just stay here, in his arms—

"Jared, is anything wrong?" Maggie stood in the doorway. She had a worried look on her face and a picnic basket in her hand.

Jared pulled away to look down at Leza. "Everything's fine now," he said to Leza, answering Maggie's question. He turned toward the older woman and a smile lit up his face. "What's this, Maggie, a peace offering?"

It was obvious that Maggie wasn't completely convinced, but she didn't press the issue. "It's too pretty a day for you two to spend it workin'. Sunshine, two young people, and a picnic by the creek sounds like a lot more fun than doin' chores. I'll have one of the boys finish the truck. You two go on and have a good time. And don't let me see your faces again till suppertime."

"Looks like we have our orders, angel," Jared said. "Feel up to it?"

Still somewhat shaken, Leza found strength in the gentleness of Jared's voice, the warmth of his hand at her elbow. "Sounds wonderful." Nearly as wonderful as the way you call me angel, she thought, forcing out everything except the feelings Jared's closeness evoked in her.

"Good," he said, picking up his shirt and tucking one end of it into his hip pocket. "I know the perfect spot. Do you ride?"

"You're talking to a native West Texan," she said with a laugh. Slowly the tension in her began to ebb. "Of course, I ride." When had being with Jared become as natural as breathing? she wondered, gladly sharing the burden of the picnic basket as they headed for the corral.

The leisurely ride to Twin Oaks on the banks of Cold Creek took just over half an hour. It was without a doubt the most beautiful, most peaceful spot Leza had ever seen. Two towering live oaks stood some twenty feet apart, their long branches dipping low to the ground, entwining so much that it was at times impossible to tell which branch belonged to which tree. One long limb swooped out over the creek, making the perfect place for a rope swing, and Leza's very active imagination quickly conjured up visions of Jared and his brother skinny-dipping there as children during the hot summertime.

Thinking of hot summertime, Leza wished she'd brought along her swimsuit. A dip in Cold Creek would be just the thing to beat the heat this afternoon. But not even the thought of the rising temperature could diminish the joy, the utter sense of contentment Leza felt at this very moment.

Lunch had come and gone two hours earlier. The fried chicken had been warm and delicious, the potato salad tart and cold, and the baked beans the best Leza could remember ever tasting. She and Jared lay side by side in the grass. Neither had spoken, or moved for that matter, since lunch and for the first time in days, Leza was absolutely content.

It had been a perfect afternoon, she realized without opening her eyes. Their conversation had vacillated between the silly and the absurd. Even so, they had discovered that they had many things in common. They both loved Irving Berlin songs, as well as country/western and oldies-but-goodies. They read and enjoyed the same authors, and while Leza confessed to a weakness for romance novels, Jared owned up to being a sucker for a well-written western. They shared ideas, even dreams, all without ever speaking of their pasts or backgrounds or families. The only thing they didn't have in common, Leza remembered, was her fondness for pizza.

"Tell me it's not true," Leza said out of the blue, still unable to believe there was someone on the face of the earth who didn't like pizza.

"Has been ever since I can remember," Jared answered just as lazily. They hadn't even mentioned pizza on their outing today, but Leza knew that somehow he had picked up on her train of thought.

She rolled her head to one side and saw him twiddling a blade of grass between his lips. Like her, he lay on his back. The only difference was that he had bunched his shirt up into a makeshift pillow, while she used her sneakers.

"Well, I think it's a shame," she chided, carefully shooing away a bumble bee that was entertaining the notion of lighting on Jared's bare belly.

"Just give me a thick, juicy T-Bone and a baked potato any day." To stress his point, he licked his lips.

"Man cannot live by steak and potatoes alone—"

"He must have Texas toast," Jared chimed in. Leza swatted him playfully and sat up, stretching her arms high overhead and wiggling her toes blissfully in the grass.

"Well, I'll bet you've never had an old-fashioned, homemade pizza. My mother makes the best—" Leza quickly cut herself short. It was the first mention either had made to anything outside of themselves. She didn't want to think about home, about her family, when her life was still so unsettled.

She changed the subject. "I can't get over how beautiful it is here. Did you and Jake spend much time here as children?"

"What makes you ask that?" Jared replied, now chewing on the blade of grass.

"Oh, I don't know. I just couldn't help thinking how wonderful it must have been for you and your brother to be raised here on Summerset." She sensed, rather than saw him tense.

"Our childhood was anything but wonderful." His words were guarded, almost bitter. "Especially after our mother was gone."

Leza silently berated herself for putting that forlorn look on his face. "I'm sorry. Were you very young when she died?"

Jared came to his feet and stood staring out across the creek. For the first time, the silence stood between them like a wall of ice. A few tense seconds passed before he answered. "She didn't die. She just left."

Even though he tried to mask it, Leza saw and felt his pain. Then, just as suddenly as it had come, the haunted look disappeared. He reached down to pull Leza to her feet.

"I want to show you something." Giving her no time to argue, he looped one arm over her shoulders. At the water's edge, he looked down, a glimmer of mischief in his gray eyes. "I've wanted to do this ever since we got here." Without warning, he swung her into his arms. Then, with a loud, "It's pay back time!" he plunged into Cold Creek, a screaming Leza clutched firmly in his arms. Jared bobbed up first, then Leza, gasping, flapping her arms, and laughing.

"That was sneaky!" she sputtered.

"Yeah, I know," Jared said with a boyish grin. "Wanna do it again?"

"Keep away," she yelled, but couldn't keep from laughing as she clambered up the sandy embankment. She hadn't laughed like this in so long, and God, it felt good. The adrenaline coursed through her as she lunged in a very unladylike fashion toward their picnic spot with Jared in hot pursuit.

She didn't see the exposed root, but she felt it when her bare foot caught on it, and she went sprawling headlong into the grass.

"Damn," she swore, falling to the ground and clutching her foot in agony.

"Let me see," Jared insisted, kneeling at her feet. Ever so gently, he moved her hands away. Leza closed her eyes and leaned back, bracing herself with her arms.

"Stupid, stupid, stupid," she chanted, rocking back and forth with the pain. "I hate it when I do something stupid like that."

Cupping the heel of her foot in one hand, Jared carefully checked each toe. His touch was gentle, sure. "Nothing's broken, but it's gonna be sore as hell for a while." His hands were as warm as the sunshine on her bare skin, his touch like nothing she'd ever known before—and on her foot, of all places.

With slow, easy strokes, he brushed away the sand. Then in the most innocent of gestures, he bent down and kissed her big toe, much as her mother had done when she was a child. But this wasn't her mother, and she wasn't a child. Mesmerized, Leza watched him run one long finger across the top of her Pampered Pink toenail and smile to himself. "Nice," was all he said. "And so very normal."

Their eyes met and in that instant Leza could hear her heart pounding in her ears, drowning out all of nature's sounds around them. Jared's eyes lazily roved over her face, coming to rest at last on her lips. Suddenly self-conscious of the tiny slit there that refused to heal, Leza dropped her gaze and broke the spell. All the old insecurities came flooding back. She felt dirty and unworthy, and when she went to move away, his fingers were there, cupping her chin, raising her head to face him.

"It doesn't matter, Leza. You're a beautiful woman, a very desirable, beautiful woman."

She should have guessed that he would know what was going through her head. "How can you say that, knowing what . . ." Her words trailed off, leaving her thought unfinished. "How would any man ever want me again?" she whispered.

"It's not your shame, angel." Jared moved closer, and again he raised her chin and tilted it at just the right angle. "I want you," he said, his voice slightly hoarse. He eased closer still. "I'm going to kiss you now." He paused only briefly, testing, it seemed, her reaction to this intimacy.

He had touched her many times over the past week, had even held her in his arms. But this was different. Still, she couldn't have moved, even if she'd wanted to, and when his lips touched hers she swallowed nervously. If she had indeed been raped—and even now a part of her still prayed there was a chance it wasn't so— how would she react to being kissed, to being touched? She braced herself. And waited. She would endure this because it was Jared and she trusted him. It was wonderful the way his lips brushed hers, retreated, then returned to nibble her top lip before moving on to the bottom one. There was a moment when he hesitated, then parted his lips to gently claim hers in a longer, sweeter, more intimate kiss. She waited, scarcely breathing. Then it was over. She opened her eyes to find him studying her. Had he sensed how anxious she had been?

"What was that, Dr. Sentell?" she asked, more than a little breathless, more than a little relieved. "Therapy?"

Jared's eyes, the color of smoldering ashes, held her hypnotized. "Let's just call it a beginning." She didn't notice the fingertips tracing across the fullest part of her lower lip. "It wasn't so bad, now was it?"

In the distance, the chow bell pealed loudly, calling them home for supper. The knot in the pit of her stomach began to loosen. "No," she admitted, taking the hand he offered her. "Not bad at all."

The night air was fresh and cool against Jared's skin, the fragrance of evening dew on the honeysuckle somehow sweeter tonight. This was his favorite time of day, when the work was all done, and he could let the events of the day slip away. He sat on the second step, sideways, his back against the railing. Not even the mosquito buzzing around his head worried him because he was too lost in thought to be bothered with it.

He couldn't remember the last time he'd enjoyed just being with a woman as much as he'd enjoyed being with Leza this afternoon. Most of the women he knew were pleasant enough, but he was careful never to let his guard down. And yet, Leza had penetrated his protective shield with nothing more than her vulnerability and a smile that did crazy things to him. He also couldn't remember when his simple plan to help her had changed to wanting her around all the time. But it had. And that scared the hell out of him.

Leza's laughter gently tugged his attention to the lighted kitchen door at his back. It was a good sign, he knew, that she was able to laugh more easily now, but the look on her face this afternoon just before he'd kissed her reminded him just how fragile she really was. Roughly he rubbed the back of his neck. What had possessed him to take such a stupid chance by kissing her? Looking back he saw how easily it might have backfired on him—and *that* scared the hell out of him, too. It would have been so easy to have lost her trust. And, he admitted, he badly wanted her to trust him.

At that very moment, she appeared at the door, the glow of the interior light silhouetting her slender frame. She had changed clothes before supper, and he'd noticed right away how her eyes picked up the soft blue-green of the sweater that clung to the generous curves of her breasts. Her white denim jeans hugged her in all the right places. He watched her hang her apron on the peg by the door, and felt a stirring somewhere deep inside of him. Who did he think he was kidding? He just plain wanted her—and wanted her to want him in return. And if she didn't want him right now, he'd just have to settle for her needing him.

He smiled in the darkness and realized that he'd been smiling a lot more often since she'd come into his life. He liked having her here, liked knowing that she needed him.

The protective instinct that had seen him through so many years slipped a little, allowing the past to creep in momentarily. He was a grown man, but the six-year-old in him couldn't forget: His mother hadn't wanted him enough to stick around, and Vietnam had changed things with Marianne. He straightened his right leg, unconsciously easing the stiffness in his hip.

"Want some company?" Leza asked from behind him.

Jared welcomed the interruption and swiveled to his right, making room for her beside him. "Dishes all done?"

"All done." She raised her head heavenward, taking in a deep breath and releasing a sigh of contentment. "This is nice. Reminds me of home."

He saw her retreating into that shell of hers, the way she did every time she was reminded of her family. But he refused to let that happen, now that they'd come this far.

"West Texas is nice," he said idly. "A little too dry

to suit me, though." Crickets chirruped in the night; cattle lowed in the distance.

"That it is," she agreed. It seemed to work; she relaxed a bit.

"Families are nice," he ventured again. "Although all I have is my brother." He paused. "Any brothers or sisters?"

"Yes," she said, her features softening. "One dear, protective, bossy older brother."

Jared chuckled softly. "Yeah, I know what you mean. What about your folks?"

"Oh, they're nice enough." She seemed to be choosing her words carefully. "No, better than that. They're great. Their only flaw is loving me too much."

"That's not possible," Jared said simply. He couldn't help thinking how different his own life might have been if his mother had cared enough to stick around.

"Yes, it is," Leza disagreed, "when you're never allowed to make a decision for yourself, when you lose your self-confidence and expect everyone else to guide you through life." Her face had become rigid, like a beautiful, inanimate piece of sculpture. "But never again." She said it so softly that he had to strain to hear.

For an awkward moment, neither said a word. Jared found himself studying the mud on his boots while Leza picked at an invisible piece of lint on her jeans.

"Well, I guess I'll call it a day." She broke the silence at last and stood on the top step. Jared rose to stand two steps lower, leaving her a head taller. Moonlight bathed her face and he saw that there was something on her mind. It was uncanny how he had learned to read her, and he suddenly knew what was troubling her.

"You'll be leaving soon, won't you?" He saw it in her eyes.

"I have to get on with my life." She spoke softly, but he heard the determination in her voice.

"I don't think you're ready," he argued gently.

She smiled down at him and he had never seen anyone look so much like an angel. "I can't stay forever."

Her statement was honest enough, but it wasn't what he wanted to hear. Slowly, he took both her hands in his, stunned at the thoughts going through his mind.

"Always would be nice."

"Always is a long time," she said wistfully.

For the first time that day, he had no idea what she was thinking when she brought one hand up to his cheek, her eyes taking in every feature of his face.

"I'm going to kiss you now." She bent down and touched her lips to his. Her kiss wasn't as experienced or as seductive as his had been, but its effect on him was immediate and explosive.

"What was that, Dr. St. Clair?" he asked. "More therapy?"

"Let's just call it progress." She left him standing in the moonlight, his pulse racing, his thoughts a jumble. He felt seventeen again, and didn't know if that was good or bad.

SEVEN

All Leza could see from the back porch was one body lying on the ground beneath Red, another leaning over the fender, and Jared kicking up dust as he traipsed back and forth between them. They were too far away for her to hear the actual words, but the tone was unmistakable: They were in definite disagreement about something.

Maggie sat in the wicker rocker to Leza's left, peeling potatoes and humming "Amazing Grace." "Looks like a case of too many cooks in the kitchen, wouldn't you say, Missy?" she said after several minutes of watching the three men squabble, curse, and generally disagree.

"Are they as angry as they sound?" Leza asked, inclining her head toward the ruckus. It didn't look as if anyone was gaining ground—least of all Red.

"It's nothin' to worry 'bout," Maggie assured her. "If John L. and Jared didn't disagree at least once a day, I'd really start to worry. It's Brad I feel sorry for. He's way outta his league with those two when it comes to swearin' and bein' just plain ornery."

Until that very moment, Leza had paid little attention to the third man, and now that she did, she saw that he wasn't much more than a boy. She'd seen him on occasion, always at distance and only briefly. If she had to guess, she'd have put him in his late teens.

It was early afternoon, and already the heat on the veranda was stifling. A ceiling fan whirled overhead, but the only real relief, Leza had learned, would come when they went back inside.

She felt a movement about her ankles and, looking down, found Hoover entertaining herself with her shoelaces. Tossing her last potato into the bowl sitting on the floor between herself and Maggie, Leza picked up Hoover and strolled to the far side of the porch to get a better view of the threesome. Another string of curses made her smile.

This was a side of Jared's nature she hadn't seen before—the impatient, cantankerous side. With her, he was always gentle and considerate. It made her suddenly aware of just how little she really knew about him. She watched the men a few minutes longer, and was relieved that Maggie had been right. They had quieted down and appeared to be discussing things more calmly now.

Hitching one hip onto the railing, she relaxed but her eyes kept straying back to Jared. She marveled at how his physical presence made her feel so many different things: protected and safe, warm and special—and something more she couldn't describe, something she'd never experienced with any man, not even Don.

As always, the thought of her ex-husband made Leza extremely uncomfortable. The only good thing they had ever truly shared, she had come to realize, had been Amy—and even the joy of Amy was tarnished by the unpleasant memory of their sex life. Leza knew she was sadly lacking in sexual experience for a twenty-seven-year-old. She had married young, barely eighteen, and had learned too late that in many ways her husband was not a patient man—especially with a nervous, virginal bride. Looking back, she was able to see that Don had never been abusive in a physical way, but when it had come to loving, he was selfish and more than a little puritanical. As a lover, he was a throwback to more straightlaced times. It hadn't taken her long to learn that if Don didn't initiate their lovemaking, there was no lovemaking. And when there was, and Leza responded too ardently, he never failed to make her feel that she had done something wrong. Her inexperience had worked to his advantage and she had endured this aspect of their marriage without questioning, without complaint. It was only after she'd decided to leave Don that she'd confided all of this to the only person she felt comfortable telling such personal things to—Steven.

Lost in her musings of the past, she leaned against the post and wondered at the differences in men. Her father, although loving and kind, could be manipulative and domineering; Don had been selfish and unfeeling; Jared was the most perplexing man she'd ever met. On the surface, he was considerate and generous to a fault, but beneath it all she sensed a reserve that should have warned her to keep her distance.

He had taken her by surprise yesterday. First on their picnic, with his perception of her thoughts, her fears. He seemed to know what she was thinking, to sense what was troubling her. And then there was his kiss. Even now, her pulse quickened at the memory of how warm, how tender his lips had felt against hers. It had been so unexpected, so spontaneous that she was glad she hadn't panicked at his touch. And yet, the biggest surprise had come last night, in this very spot. She relived those few moments in the darkness. Always would be nice, he had said. Had he meant it literally, or had she misinterpreted him completely?

This is crazy, she thought. He couldn't have been serious. They hardly knew each other, and besides, she had a new life to build.

Whether he'd been serious or not, those words had frightened her into action. After leaving him, she'd gone straight upstairs and called Steven. She'd had every intention of telling him that her car was ready and she would be on her way to Rosemont the next morning, but the instant she heard his voice, she backed out.

It had been almost two weeks since Jared had brought her to Summerset, and still she wasn't ready to face her brother. Obviously, she wasn't yet strong enough to stand her ground with him. She hadn't exaggerated when she'd told Jared that Steven was protective and bossy. She wanted her own apartment as soon as possible. Steven made no secret that he wanted her to stay with him indefinitely. She wanted to concentrate on her work. He had a calendar of social events scheduled for her. Steven meant well, but if she went to him now while she was this insecure, it would just end up being a replay of her very docile, very obedient past.

So, she'd cheerfully told Steven that the garage had ordered the wrong parts, that she still had things to see and do, and that she'd be back in touch in a few days. In granting herself a reprieve where Steven was concerned, she had inadvertently placed herself more soundly in Jared's keeping. It wouldn't bother her so much if she only knew a little more about him.

Again her eyes were drawn to Jared, who had stopped pacing. "Maggie?" She hesitated, almost changing her mind. There were things she had to know, but did she have the right to pry into his past?

"What is it, Missy?"

Making up her mind, Leza turned and looked at the older woman. "Tell me about Jared."

Maggie laid her knife aside and seemed to consider Leza's request. At last, she patted the rocker beside her. "Come sit by me." When Leza did as she was asked, Maggie began, "It's no secret that I like to talk, and even though Jared's life is nobody's business but his own, I got me a gut feelin' 'bout you." Her smile was warm, grandmotherly, and Leza felt much easier. "What is it you want to know?"

"Oh, I don't know," Leza said, hesitating again. "Everything, I guess. Tell me about his mother. Jared mentioned her yesterday, said she left when he was little."

That seemed to surprise Maggie. She looked thoughtful, then leaned back in her rocker. Focusing her attention on the clouds in the clear Texas sky, she began to rock slowly back and forth. "I didn't know Roger and Victoria Sentell very well, but rumor had it that she'd run away from her family in New Orleans to marry him. They wound up a few years later in Kilgore with two small boys." Here she paused long enough to look at Leza. "I'm not makin' excuses for her, mind you, but Victoria wasn't cut out to be the wife of an East Texas roughneck any more'n Roger was meant to be anythin' else. That's just the way it was. Anyway, one day she just up and left." She paused and sighed deeply. "Why she didn't take Jake and Jared is anybody's guess."

"Were they very young?"

" 'Bout six or seven, if I remember right."

"How sad," Leza said, her heart breaking for two small boys who must have thought their world had fallen apart. "Didn't Roger try to find her?"

Maggie's face went rigid. "Roger was sick at heart, but that was no excuse for the way he acted. At first he didn't do nothin' but drink and gamble, then he started chasin' ever'thin' in skirts.'' Leza had never heard Maggie speak harshly about anyone before. ''It was a cryin' shame the way he left them boys alone to fend for themselves. They had a terrible time livin' down the reputation of oil field trash, but they worked hard and did a darned good job of takin' care of themselves and that worthless father of theirs.''

''And Roger?''

''Finally drank hisself to death with two teenage sons watchin' him. Jake adjusted 'bout as well as could be expected, but Jared . . .'' She paused again, this time glancing across the way at Jared. ''. . . Well, I think Jared just decided that no woman would ever do to him what Victoria had done to Roger.''

Intuition told Leza there was more to the story. ''And we all know what happens when you vow never to.''

''Yep, you guessed it,'' Maggie said with a wry little smile. ''He met Marianne Prescott, the prettiest, richest, most spoiled girl in town.''

Leza felt a little silly at the pang of jealousy stabbing through her. ''What happened?'' she had to know.

''Well, Marianne's daddy was the mayor, and he wasn't too happy 'bout his precious daughter marryin' a low-life oilpatch hand. But like most little girls, Marianne knew just how to work her daddy, and it wasn't long till she and Jared were plannin' a double weddin' with Jake and Becky.''

Leza remembered Jared telling her that first day that he lived alone. What had happened to his spoiled little rich girl?

''Uncle Sam had other plans, though,'' Maggie added before Leza could ask the question. ''Jake was inducted into the Military Police and Jared was shipped off to Vietnam.''

''Becky waited for Jake, but when Jared was sent home with a busted-up hip and little chance of walkin' again, Marianne called off the weddin' and married the boy her daddy'd been pushin' at her for months.''

So much made sense to Leza now. The sad, guarded look in Jared's eyes that he tried to mask whenever she caught him looking at her. The way he had painstakingly replaced the bird's nest so that the mother wouldn't detect his tampering. His mother's desertion and Marianne's betrayal had both left their marks on him.

"Somethin' inside Jared changed then." Maggie didn't seem to notice that Leza's attention had strayed. "He became determined—" she cut herself short. "No, he became *obsessed* with the idea of makin' somethin' of hisself. It was like he decided that very day that he wasn't worthy of love and would just do without it." Maggie looked so sad that Leza wanted to comfort her. "So, with Jake's help, he suffered through months of therapy to get his leg back in shape. By that time, Jake and Becky had a little one on the way. All Jared had was his bad memories and a determination to put the past behind him. They worked like Trojans to get J & J runnin' smooth, and when they did, Jake decided he wanted to be a lawman. He became a silent partner, lettin' Jared run the show while he got on with his own life. That's about the time Mack showed up. Like the man or not, I'll have to admit that he really stood behind Jared. Helped him out of many a bind.''

"I'm not following you," Leza interrupted. "Who's Mack?"

"Sorry," Maggie apologized. "Mack's an old Army buddy. If it hadn't been for him, Jared would be either dead or a prisoner of war. He owes Mack his life, and I think Mack uses that—" Again she cut herself off. "You'll have to excuse me. I get carried away sometimes when it comes to Jared." The faraway look in Maggie's eyes disappeared when she looked at Leza. "I worry that he'll never let hisself become involved again.

I don't think he realizes to this day how driven he's become—or how lonely he is.''

Leza couldn't imagine a man like Jared Sentell lonely. "Surely there's someone special in his life?" she asked aloud, surprising herself.

"There would be if Marianne had any say in it," Maggie told her. "That woman's been pesterin' Jared ever since her husband died this past November.''

"Hi ya, Maggie," a young voice interrupted. Leza glanced up to see the man Maggie had called Brad walking up to the back steps. "Got anything good'n cold to drink?" he asked, his greeting as cheerful as his broad smile. Leza had guessed right about his age; he was in his mid to late teens. His sandy-blond hair fell about his face when he tipped his hat to her with a courteous, "Ma'am."

Maggie stood and smoothed her apron. "What'll it be, iced tea or lemonade?"

"Considering the mood those two are in," Brad said with a glance over his shoulder at John L. and Jared, "lemonade might just sweeten 'em up."

"I won't tell 'em you said that," Maggie teased on her way to the kitchen.

"Thanks," Brad called back, shifting from one foot to the other. He seemed a little uncomfortable and Leza didn't know what to say.

"So," she ventured, "how's it coming along?"

He looked blank for a second, then he caught her meaning. "Oh, the 'Vette," he said, obviously relieved to have something to say. "Shouldn't be too much longer." As if on cue, Red fired up, and Brad joined John L. and Jared in a whoop of victory.

"Looks like you're back in business," Brad said, but his excitement waned when he was face-to-face with her again. She almost felt sorry for him as he started to fidget again, lowering his eyes to the ground.

"Hey," he blurted out, "I like your license plate. PAID 4. That's real cute." He met her gaze for the first time. "Did you know they expired last month?"

"No, I didn't. Thanks for telling me." She'd been so busy planning for her trip that she'd overlooked getting her vehicle registration tended to. She made a mental note to take care of it the next day.

"Listen," Brad broke into her thoughts. She looked up to find him staring at his boots. "I'm awful sorry 'bout the way me and the boys acted on the road that night."

It was Leza's turn to look blank. "Have we met before?" she asked, alarmed by the uneasy feeling that was beginning to build inside her.

"How 'bout a hand here?" Maggie called from the door. Brad looked grateful for the interruption and bounded up the four steps to relieve her of the tray and three glasses of lemonade.

"Tell Jared to pick up the phone in the barn. Mack's on the line." Maggie glanced from Brad to Leza.

"Sure thing." Carefully balancing his load, Brad headed for the barn.

"Do you know Brad, Missy?" Maggie didn't miss much.

"I don't think so." Leza tried to ignore the hard knot forming in the pit of her stomach. Was it happening again? She braced herself for another flash of recall. Nothing happened, but before she could breathe a sigh of relief, she asked, "Does he have a friend named Evan?" Where had the name come from?

"His cousin." Maggie looked as surprised as Leza felt, and when she took Leza's hands in her own, Leza couldn't look her in the eye. "You'd better tell Jared, Missy—"

"No!" Leza pulled free and stepped away. *Don't panic*, she told herself. *Take it easy.* "No," she said more calmly. "What can I tell him, Maggie. I didn't remember anything, the name just . . . came to mind. And besides, Brad's just a boy. He wouldn't hurt anyone."

"I didn't say I thought Brad was responsible, Missy. But what if he was there? What if he saw somethin'?"

"Maggie, don't," Leza pleaded. "It's too soon. I'm not ready—"

"Not ready for what?"

Leza jumped at the sound of Jared's voice. She dropped Maggie's hand and whirled around to find him at the steps, not five feet away.

"Not ready for another trip into Rosemont." She turned again to Maggie. "Maybe tomorrow." *Please*, she mouthed silently.

"Whatever you say, Missy. Now, what was it Mack wanted?" she asked Jared, neatly maneuvering the subject from Leza.

Jared looked like he wanted to pursue it further, but thankfully, he didn't. "He'll be here for supper, Maggie," he said instead. "Sorry for the short notice, but he has a report we have to go over before he leaves for Galveston tomorrow morning." His eyes hadn't left Leza since she turned to find him behind her. He had come to know her too well, she feared, and she wasn't up to fending off his questions right now.

"I'm going to have to beg off on our horseback ride, Jared," she said a bit too abruptly. "I'm a little tired."

She didn't wait for an answer. With the turmoil going on inside of her, she wasn't sure she could carry on a casual conversation.

Think! she commanded herself when she was alone in her room. *Try to remember!* But the harder she tried, the more frightened she became, and the more frightened she became, the less she was able to reason. She was no good to herself like this. She had to calm down. She fell across the bed and willed her mind to clear. Just when things seemed to be on an even keel, she thought, closing her eyes and taking several deep breaths, something would happen to knock her for a loop. But she was getting stronger, more in control everyday. She could handle this, she told herself, finally beginning to relax. She took another deep, cleansing breath, and was asleep in a matter of minutes.

"You should have called me in on this at the very beginning, Jared." Jacob Sentell paced the length of Jared's study with long, sure strides, a service revolver strapped to his hip, his brown khaki uniform blending nicely with the decor of the room.

"I told you, Jake, the lady was in no shape to give any kind of statement—to you or to anyone," Jared defended himself. He had considered calling his brother that very first night, but every time he'd picked up the phone, Leza's words popped into his brain. *Please, I can't stay here. He'll find out if I stay.* She'd had her reasons, and he simply hadn't been able to do anything that would upset her even more.

"I know what you told me." Jake glared across the room at his brother. "But I *am* the sheriff of this county, you know. And a crime was committed. You could have trusted me enough—"

"It didn't have anything to do with trust, damn it." Jared was close to losing his temper, and that wouldn't do anyone any good. Deep inside he knew Jake wasn't really angry, just upset that Jared hadn't come to him with his problem. Not only were they brothers—twins—they were friends. He couldn't remember there ever being the slightest bit of sibling rivalry between them. They had shared everything during their childhood—clothes and food, the good and the bad, the laughter and the tears. This was different, and Jake would just have to understand.

"I did what I thought was best, Jake, just like I did today. She doesn't know I've talked to Brad or that I called you." *And she's going to be mad as hell when she finds out I tried to talk to Maggie behind her back.* Still, he had to follow through on this. There was, after all, a rapist on the loose. Brad had been there and he might know something important.

Almost as though the thought of the boy had conjured him up, Brad stepped through the open door. "Dad," he greeted Jake, then nodded to Jared.

"Have a seat, Brad," Jared told his nephew. "Now, tell us what happened."

Brad glanced up at the identical twins towering above him. If things weren't so serious, Jared thought, the look on the boy's face might have made him laugh. To have to face his father with this was bad enough, especially when he was the sheriff, but to have a carbon copy glaring down at him, too, had to be intimidating as hell. He nudged his brother and they both sat down; Jake beside his son with the door to their backs, Jared facing them from behind the desk. Brad seemed to relax a little.

"Well, sir," he began, "it was early Saturday evening, just past dark, and me and the boys had finished baling and stacking the hay. We were hot and tired and thirsty, and looking forward to a swim in the clay pit. We'd had a couple of beers—"

"Where'd you get the booze?" Jake wanted to know.

"Later," Jared butted in. Begrudgingly, Jake nodded agreement.

Brad cleared his throat nervously. "Anyway," he went on, "we headed for the clay pit when we saw this lady and her red Corvette in the roadside park. She was having car trouble, so we stopped." He looked down at his boots. "We tried to talk her into joining us, but she wasn't interested in partying. Then some dude stopped and we left."

"You just left?" both men asked in unison.

"Well, sir, we were being kinda rowdy, and I think we kinda scared her," Brad admitted. "And besides, we were kinda afraid of being caught with a cooler of beer. A couple of the guys ain't quite old enough—"

"Like you, Brad?" Jake obviously had a bone to pick with his oldest son.

Jared knew the boy was nervous, but if he used the word "kinda" one more time, he was going to thump him good and proper. The brothers looked at each other and shook their heads.

"Did you get a good look at him or his car?" Jake continued the inquisition.

"No, sir, we didn't. We'd stopped in front of her. He'd pulled up behind her, and his headlights was on bright. We couldn't see nothing." Brad looked from one sober face to the other. "We didn't do nothing wrong, did we? We didn't mean no harm. We figured he'd help her and we'd get on with our party."

For the past few minutes, it had been all Jared could do to keep from snatching his nephew to his feet and throttling him for his part in Leza's troubles, but the look on the youngster's face checked his temper.

"You couldn't have known, son," Jake consoled the boy. "But *you* and *me*," he stressed the words, "we're gonna have a *good, long* talk when we get home."

"Yes, sir." Brad chanced a glance at his uncle. "Jared, if I'd known . . ."

"It's all right, Brad." Jared was finding it hard to keep from venting his frustration on Brad.

"Damn," Jake swore, "we don't know any more now than we did before."

"The hell we don't." The room had suddenly grown

cold. Jared stood and briskly rubbed his right thigh. "We know that the boys scared the living daylights out of her, and some animal took advantage of that fear. I've come to know her pretty well, Jake, and she wouldn't get into a car with just anybody." A sound drew his attention toward the open door. "Leza," he called as she bolted down the hallway without answering.

"Stay here," Jared barked to Jake and Brad, then sprang into action. It took some doing, but he finally caught her on the front porch.

"Didn't you hear me?" He grabbed her by the arm and spun her to face him.

"I heard everything." She was angry, and didn't try to hide it. "How could you do this to me, Jared? You had no right. It was my decision to make, and I wasn't ready."

"I hoped Brad could tell us something to help us get a lead on that bastard. We can't just leave him on the loose to rape someone else." She tried to pull away, but he tightened his grip. "The sheriff is my brother, Leza. I'd trust him with my life." Relaxing his hold, he held her at arm's length. "I trust him to help you," he said, his voice slightly husky.

"I wouldn't care if he was *my* brother, Jared. I can't talk about this now. I don't know anything to tell."

"That may have been true yesterday," he argued, "but Brad was there that night. It's not much to go on, but it's a start."

Still not convinced, Leza squirmed against his grasp. "I heard all Brad had to say, and it still doesn't make any sense to me—"

"Can't you see what's happening?" He shook her roughly, then rubbed her arms where he'd held her too tightly. "It's coming back little by little, and I don't know what else to do to help you."

She seemed to sense his helplessness, and he saw that

it frightened her. Hoping to take away her fear, to fill her with his own strength, he pulled her into his arms.

"You need help, angel—counseling from professionals, people who know what they're doing. There's a group in Rosemont I want— "

"*You* want!" Leza shouted, tearing away from his embrace with a strength that surprised him. "You're not my father, you're not my husband, and since it's my life we're talking about, it doesn't make a whole hell of a lot of difference what you want." Before he could stop her, she was at the bottom of the front steps, glaring up at him. "Now, if you have no objections, I'm going for that ride. Alone."

His first impulse was to go after her and shake some sense into her. Intuitively, though, he knew that was exactly the wrong way to handle her. He had seen her at her worst and at her best. She might be stubborn, but in the end he was certain she would come around to doing what had to be done.

EIGHT

By the time Leza reached Twin Oaks it was dusk. Summer Star stood grazing at the water's edge while Leza sat on the ground some distance away and fought to bring her emotions under control. It seemed an impossible task, however, since the events of the afternoon insisted on replaying over and over in her mind.

She hadn't meant to fall asleep, but the episode with Brad had left her emotionally drained. Awakening later, she started downstairs to help Maggie with supper when she'd heard voices in the study—Jared's and Brad's. Realizing they were talking about her, she paused to listen.

Brad and another man—the sheriff, she now knew—were sitting with their backs to the door. Jared was seated behind his desk, too involved in Brad's story to notice her until she accidentally brushed against the coatrack.

Was it the chill of the evening air caressing her cheek that made her shiver, or the memory of their heated exchange on the front steps? In frustration, she pounded the earth with both fists.

She was angry—no, damn it, she was furious with Jared. How dare he! She found it ironic that just last night she had told him how important it was for her to make her own decisions. Still, he'd decided to interfere. She cursed herself for having fled to her room, for leaving him free to poke around until he figured out what had happened to upset her. She couldn't imagine Maggie breaking her word. Obviously, Jared had concluded that Brad had said or done something to upset her.

Yes, she was angry, but it was more than that. She was deeply disappointed. She and Jared had spent many hours together since his return from Houston, and she had been certain they'd become more than just two people thrown together by circumstances.

Sighing deeply, she leaned against the base of the oak, the same tree beneath which he had kissed her only yesterday. Remembering his kiss and the way it had affected her, she closed her eyes and relived those moments when his lips had touched hers—softly, tenderly, demanding nothing and giving so much. She had sensed no aggression, no threat in his closeness, and she hadn't wanted the kiss to end. Would remembering that terrible night take away the only pleasant thing to happen to her in recent memory? Would she still respond to Jared if it all came back? Until now, she hadn't known how much she had to lose. Why was he was pushing her to remember?

Summer Star drifted closer and nuzzled her gently. It was growing darker by the minute and Leza knew she should go, but there were just too many things rattling around inside her head. She had to collect her wits, plan her next move before someone else did it for her.

She took a deep breath and waited for her mind to clear. It took awhile, but when it did, one thought stood out—from the very beginning Jared had done nothing that hadn't been in her best interests. Questioning Brad and calling in the sheriff were no different. Jared had done the only thing he could—the right thing.

Since she was doing all this soul-searching, she had to admit something else. No matter how unintentionally, she *had* encouraged Jared's protectiveness from the very beginning. First, by staying at Summerset after his return from Houston, and then by allowing him to become such a vital part of her life. Like it or not, she was as much to blame as Jared for what had seemed to be his high-handed interference.

She came to her feet and stared across Cold Creek, much as Jared had done the day of their picnic. Yes, it was definitely time to do something, even if it was wrong. The partial loss of her memory had made her overly cautious, fearful of doing anything without serious thought. But Brad's presence that night put a whole new perspective on things. It would be difficult, but with Brad's help, perhaps they could come up with some answers.

Once they did, she decided with a heavy heart, it would be time to leave Summerset—and the man she had come to depend on too much.

Jared swore beneath his breath as he fumbled with Summer Storm's cinch. He shouldn't have listened to Maggie. He'd agreed at the time only because he'd known she was right. Leza needed some time alone, and he knew that she couldn't get lost. Summer Star knew her way home well enough to make it back even after dark.

But that had been over three hours ago, and he was sick with worry. So worried, in fact, that he'd broken his own rule and had a third bourbon with Mack during their meeting. He hadn't been himself all evening, and even Mack, the most efficient, cool-headed person he knew, had found it so difficult to deal with Jared's bad temper that he'd called the meeting short himself. It was damned frustrating not to be able to concentrate on his work, and although Mack had a knack for rubbing him the wrong way at times, Jared was relieved that his old Army buddy was here to handle the situation in Galveston.

Just as Jared secured the cinch and swung into the saddle, Leza led Summer Star into the barn. To him, she looked like heaven in faded blue jeans and a Dallas Cowboys T-shirt. Relief washed over him, and dismounting he gathered her into his arms. She returned his embrace, and he knew that all was forgiven. "I was just on my way to Twin Oaks," he whispered against her hair.

The smile she had for him made his heart race. "That's where you would have found me."

Never had he wanted to kiss her as badly as he did at this very moment. Slowly he lowered his head to hers. He wasn't surprised when she stepped out of his embrace, but knowing that he was moving too fast didn't keep his heart from feeling as empty as his arms. It had been a long time in coming, and now that he had found love, he wouldn't let anything stand in his way. One day she would want him. It was just a matter of time.

They unsaddled and fed their mounts in silence. Neither of them wanted mere words to break the closeness they had just shared.

Together they left the barn, but before they'd gone half the distance to the house, Leza stopped him with a touch. "I did a lot of thinking while I was gone, Jared." She didn't pull away when he reached out to tuck one unruly curl behind her ear. "I didn't like your method, but you were right. Don't smile at me like that. I can't think when you do." She stepped back, turning away from him, then faced him again. "I'll talk with your brother and Brad tomorrow. I can't get on with my life until I've put all this behind me.''

"Good." Jared felt a rush of relief. "I've been waiting for the right time to give you this." He reached into his shirt pocket and pulled out a slip of paper. "It's the address and phone number of the Rape Crisis Center in Rosemont." The icy look that froze her features told him louder than words that he'd ruffled her feathers again. He stepped back and raised both hands outward. "It's only a suggestion.''

Leza hesitated briefly, almost as if she were weighing his words. "I know you're right," she said at last, taking the paper and stuffing it into her own pocket. "But don't push me."

Never had he admired anyone as much as he admired her at that very moment. She was scared—putting herself on the line without knowing how it was going to turn out.

"I'll try not to, but remember that I'll be with you, angel, every step of the way.''

He sensed that she wanted to say something more, but instead she looped her arm around his waist. Casually Jared put his arm about her shoulders, and they strolled the rest of the way to the house in companionable silence.

They stepped into the kitchen and Jared flipped on the light. "Hungry?" he asked, knowing that Maggie had put a covered plate in the oven for Leza.

"Enough to eat pizza," she answered, the teasing light in her eyes warming him through and through.

"There's just no accounting for taste," he said as he opened the oven door and took out a foil-covered plate while Leza took two glasses from the cupboard.

A very domestic scene, he thought, clearing away the ashtray and papers he and Mack had left strewn on the tabletop. And a very nice scene. This wasn't like him at all, but then he hadn't much liked the man he'd become over the years. Driven by his past, he had laughed little and loved less. Now there was Leza, and there was hope after all.

He was so caught up in his musings that he wasn't aware of the stillness in the room until he glanced up to see Leza. She had filled both glasses with iced tea, and had just set them down when her face lost all color. He thought he heard her breath start coming in short, jagged bursts. A sudden sense of dread filled him when she began to move her head slowly from side to side. He didn't know what was happening, but he'd sell his soul to stop it.

"What's that smell?" Her voice cracked. Her face grew even whiter, more drawn. Her eyes, those wonderful blue-green eyes that looked at him with such trust, grew wide and bright with fear. Not even that first day when she'd awakened in his bedroom had he seen her so stricken.

He tested the air. "Pot roast and greens," he said, moving around the table toward her. "Maybe tobacco." If only he could hold her . . .

She shrank away, her features contorted in anguish. "No," she whispered, shaking her head as if to rid herself of some vile thing. "Not now. Please, not now . . ." Before he could get to her, she fell to her knees, clutching her head with both hands. He was beside her on the floor, trying to hold her, trying to give comfort. She wrenched away, then threw herself back into his arms. "Make it go away," she pleaded, grabbing his shirt savagely. "He's here . . . inside my head . . . I can see him hurting me. . . . Oh, Jared, I remember it all!" She looked up at him, her face filled with agony. "Help me, Jared. Make it go away. I can't deal with this yet."

He'd known all along that this moment would come,

had studied all the pamphlets, knew all the right words to say. But now that the time had come, he felt helplessly, pitifully unprepared. He shouldn't have been surprised when she came up on her knees to kiss him urgently, but she took him off guard when she demanded, "Make love to me, Jared. You can make *him* go away."

He knew she was hurting, and God, it was the hardest thing he'd ever had to do, but gently, firmly, he moved her away from him.

"No, Leza," he told her. "I'll listen if you need to talk, but—"

"Talk?" she said in disbelief, then laughed aloud. He saw she was close to hysteria. "Talk is the last thing I want now," she said so calmly that it stunned him. It took only a moment for him to see that she was struggling to regain her composure. He could have cried for the suffering, for the desperation he saw in her eyes.

Over the weeks, he'd learned that each rape victim reacted differently when it came to the physical aspect of loving. While one might shrink away from the idea of making love with her partner, another might want reassurances in the form of a physical relationship. This was simply Leza's way of telling herself that in time she would be able to cope with not only the memories, but with the physical act itself. Whatever she was feeling, Jared knew that she needed anything now but a lover.

At long last, she made her way back to his arms and he felt her go limp against him. Emotionally and physically exhausted, she clung to him and sobbed softly. He lifted her in his arms and carried her upstairs. Carefully, he sat her on the edge of her bed and removed her shoes and jeans. Just as he was about to move away to find her nightgown, she reached out for him.

"Don't leave me," she whispered in the darkness,

taking his hand and pulling him down to lie beside her. She smelled of wind and sunshine and honeysuckle, and he hadn't the strength or the will to pull away from her. He eased closer and felt her trembling begin to subside. He would just hold her until she fell asleep, he told himself, give her whatever comfort he could, if only for a little while. Even after her breathing became steady and rhythmic, though, he didn't leave her, couldn't force himself to go. Instead, he buried his face in her hair and held her close. She fit so perfectly alongside of him. Nothing had ever felt so right, so perfect, he thought, breathing in her scent as he, too, drifted into a deep, exhausted sleep.

Leza couldn't get close enough to the warmth lying next to her. Opening her eyes, she saw Jared, fully dressed, except for his boots. He was sleeping soundly. Still groggy with sleep, she shivered and drew her left leg up and across him, then shifted her body closer. He smelled as he always did, of outdoors and spicy cologne, but there was something else, something she couldn't quite get a handle on. She took a deep breath and finally recognized the distinct scent of bourbon.

Her heart began to pound beneath her breast when she remembered how suddenly the memories had returned and how vehemently she had pleaded with Jared to make the memories go away. What if he hadn't been so brave and steadfast, had made love to her as she demanded? Would she have been able to follow through, or would she have fallen apart again and never known the feel of his body next to hers like this?

Even in her state of semi-sleep, Leza was struck by the foolishness of wanting Jared to make love to her as a cure for anything. Yes, he had been her strength through all of this, but she was just coming to realize that that wasn't all he had become to her.

His hand moved slowly up the length of her arm to rest on her shoulder. This time the shiver that went through her wasn't from the chill of the night. She had wanted him to make love to her, she realized, simply because she wanted him to love her.

Sometime in the night she turned to him—all woman and warmth, and snuggled closer, breathing his name against his skin. Her body lay partially across his, and it was impossible to tell if it was his heart or hers pounding against his ribs. Her lips brushed his neck; her words fell softly near his ear.

"Jared, I need you."

They were probably the sweetest words he had ever heard, but he stilled the fingers fumbling with the buttons of his shirt by pressing them firmly to his chest. Despite the effect of the alcohol he'd consumed earlier, he knew that if he took her now, while she was hurt and confused, she might never forgive him. He wanted her, but not at that cost.

Moonlight filtered through the window to bathe the room in a soft, hazy glow. He looked down into her sleepy eyes, eyes filled with longing, and his resolve began to crumble. He hadn't expected her to take his hand and place it on her breast, but she did, and he swallowed the groan that rose in his throat. Even through the thin fabric of her T-shirt, she felt like nothing he'd ever known before.

"God, Leza, do you know what you're doing?" He couldn't believe it was his voice—so shaky, so full of wanting. Again she kissed him—such a hungry, urgent kiss that he could scarcely breathe. Her lips tasted of tears, and all he wanted was to wipe away her pain, to make the past go away.

"Yes," she whispered, arching boldly against him, urging him with each move to love her. "If I stop now,

I'll never know . . .'' This time when her lips found his, he knew he was lost.

Her hands fumbled with the buttons on his shirt, then his jeans while he suppressed the urge to do it for her. Patiently he waited while she stripped him of every article of clothing he wore. Then he sat up and lifted her shirt off over her head. The sight of her took his breath away. He had seen her undressed before, that long ago night when she'd needed help with the bath she'd insisted on, but he hadn't noticed then how perfect her breasts were, how smooth and unblemished her skin was. He wanted her to feel what he was feeling, but when he rolled to his side, pinning her to the mattress, she stopped him with a single word.

''No,'' she said, a note of urgency warning him to move more slowly. Instinct told him she needed to be the aggressor, to be the one in control. He paused, searching her features for any sign of fear as she gently pushed him onto his back.

Silhouetted above him in the darkness, she hesitated before cautiously laying her hand on his bare chest. It seemed forever before she moved, as though she were testing not only for her reactions to touching him, but his reactions to being touched.

He waited, scarcely daring to breathe, then raised his hand to caress her cheek. He felt her smile against his palm, and then, without a word, she slowly moved her hand across the breadth of his chest. His sudden intake of breath when her fingers wandered lower across his abdomen startled her, and she pulled away.

''It's okay, angel,'' he said with a jagged breath, taking her hand and guiding it back to where it had been. It seemed to be all the encouragement she needed. She moved over him, her hair and her breasts brushing against his skin as she trailed tiny kisses across his shoulders, his neck.

He couldn't remember ever having to suppress his healthy appetite for the fairer sex. He'd had his share of physical relationships, and with women more experienced than Leza. But never had he known anything as exciting as the way she touched him, kissing him, or as provocative as the way she moved to straddle him.

Leza awoke at daybreak, her head pounding as fiercely as her heart. She sat up slowly. The sight of Jared's clothing in a crumpled heap on the floor beside her own made her grimace.

It hadn't been a dream. It had really happened.

She closed her eyes against the memory of Jared pulling her close just before sunrise, whispering something about his brother being a pain. His body had been warm, his touch gentle, and she hadn't wanted him to leave. He had chuckled softly, then with a sweet, lingering kiss promised to hurry back as he slipped from her bed and out of her room.

Drawing an unsteady breath, Leza leaned against the headboard and with trembling fingers began to massage her temples. So many things kept tumbling around inside her head—the total recall of the rape and her violent reaction, her aggressiveness as Jared's lover and his tender responses.

Her nerves were frazzled and she was beginning to seriously question her sanity. Even so, she was aware enough to know that something had triggered her memory last night. But no matter how she tried, she couldn't pinpoint that something. Too many other things kept sidetracking her. Why had she lost control so completely? And why had she forced Jared into making love to her when the thought of sex should have scared her witless?

With total recall of the rape, Leza experienced a host of emotions she wasn't prepared for. And questions she hadn't considered before dominated her thoughts. Had the assault been her fault? Could she have prevented it? Most important of all, had she been responsible in any way?

"No!" She pounded the bed with tightly clenched fists. Again she rubbed her temples and tried to keep from thinking. But then thoughts of the night before flooded her tormented mind and she knew that she *had* been to blame for last night. Jared had been willing to keep the memories at bay by simply holding her, but she had forced their lovemaking. What had she been trying to prove? That she was capable of a physical relationship with a man? That she wouldn't fall apart if a man touched her? That she deserved to be loved?

And loved she had been. Memories of her night in Jared's arms invaded her mind. She'd slept peacefully after that first frantic loving until he'd awakened her with kisses, to love her again, slowly, thoroughly, as a woman was meant to be loved by a man. It had been so wonderful, so perfect, that even in the light of day, she could find no flaw with their lovemaking—until she remembered how demanding she had been as Jared's lover. Just as quickly, she remembered that Jared hadn't seemed to mind, had, in fact, encouraged her, unlike Don, who—

Unbidden and unwanted, memories of past hurt blocked out all thought of Jared. "Ladies do not make the first move," Don reproached her whenever she wanted to be close. He had drilled this and other archaic notions into her head from the time she was a frightened, eighteen-year-old bride. She had been so inexperienced with men that she'd finally stopped questioning her lack of real involvement in their sex life. Since she had never been one to discuss her private life with anyone, she'd simply assumed that all men felt the same as Don about a woman's sexual role.

But not all men are Jared Sentell, she realized abruptly, dismissing the bad thoughts and slipping from bed. It was time to put the pain and fear behind her. Time to get on with living. Jared would be back soon, and she wanted to be able to look him in the eye and see exactly how last night had affected him. To do that, she wanted to look her best.

In the bathroom, she stood before the mirror, completely naked, and for the first time in days really looked at herself. To tell the truth, she had never given much thought to what others called her natural beauty. She stood erect, turning from side to side, and wished for the thousandth time that she were taller. That was normal, though. Didn't all her taller friends fret about their height, and wish that they could lose an inch or two?

To her way of thinking, her eyes were her best feature; large and wide set, they reminded her of her father's. Her lips, she decided, were her mother's, and her hair—well, what could she say? Shoving the unruly curls from her face, she grimaced. The color was nice enough—ebony, her friends called it—but the only way she had found to control the stubborn mass of curls was to keep it shoulder length and layered about her face. Its sole virtue was that it took so little time to style. Just a quick shampoo and comb-out and she was ready for almost anything.

In stark contrast to the darkness of her hair and the vibrant blue-green of her eyes, her skin was fair and unblemished—usually.

She leaned closer to the mirror to inspect the slight reddening around her mouth, and lower on her neck. Another flush of color that had nothing to do with the whisker burn crept over her when she remembered Jared's passion during the night.

Her gaze traveled lower, and Leza found herself

considering her body as Jared might, remembering as she did how it felt when Jared touched her. Her breasts, though small, were full and firm; her abdomen, flat; and her waist curved into a generous fullness at her hips. She knew that she had given Jared as much pleasure as he had given her, but would he find her as appealing in the clear light of day?

Don't be silly, she chided herself, and briskly washed her face and combed her hair. Quickly dressing for the day, she made her bed and folded Jared's jeans and shirt, then took them to his room.

Voices outside drew her to the balcony, and across the way she saw Jared, astride Summer Star, just leaving the barn. It didn't strike her that he was riding the mare instead of Summer Storm. She only knew that a morning ride would be the perfect way to start the day.

On impulse, she waved and called out, "Jared, wait for me and I'll—" Her words died on her lips when he turned her way. The look on his face, even at this distance, made her heart stop beating. It was as though he were seeing a stranger when he touched his fingertips to the brim of his hat, then turned stiffly and rode away.

She fought the urge to turn and run. What had happened? Earlier he had been nothing but loving and warm. This was a Jared she had never seen before, his features rock-hard, his eyes filled with . . . what? Don's face jumped into sharp focus, bringing to mind all the times he had disapproved of her, all the nights she had cried herself to sleep because she thought she had displeased him.

How could she have been so stupid?

Fighting back the tears, she raced along the balcony to her own room and hurriedly began to toss her things into her bags. She loved Jared too much to stay when he was obviously regretting last night. How could she face him and the contempt she was sure to find in his eyes?

Bags in tow, she made her way down the stairs. She was grateful that today was wash day and that Maggie was hanging clothes on the line on the other side of the house.

Just as she reached the back door she remembered Hoover. Stopping to search for her, she found the kitten curled into a tight ball asleep beside the dryer. She scooped up the sleeping cat and raced for her car, which was parked near the end of the drive. The keys, thankfully, were in the ignition, and as the engine fired to life, she sped away from the man who would never know how much she loved him.

NINE

It never rained that Jared didn't think of Leza, and October had been one rainy day after the next. Today was no exception.

". . . and you haven't heard a word I've said, Jared." Mack Thomasson glared down at the chief executive of Sentell Enterprises. "In fact," he pressed his point, "you haven't heard much anyone's said for the past six months."

Jared didn't bother answering. Instead, he turned away from the window and took his seat behind his desk. He leaned back in the plush office chair and glanced distractedly in Mack's direction. Six months? Had it been that long? In less than a heartbeat, the events of that last day with Leza filled his mind—and his heart. Their argument before she'd fled on horseback, the fear he'd seen on her face when the memories returned, and way she'd felt in his arms.

"I'll be damned," Mack swore. "You've done it again." Irritated, he tossed the file he'd been trying to discuss for the past ten minutes onto Jared's desk.

The folder landed with a thud, drawing Jared's attention back to the business at hand. It was obvious by the way Mack shoved his hands deep into his pockets that he was angry, an emotion he rarely, if ever, showed. In Jared's estimation, Mack was the most cool-headed person he'd ever known. No, he revised his thought instantly, calculating was a better description of his associate's nature.

"If I didn't know you better, Jared, I'd swear there's a woman—" Mack stopped in mid-sentence when Jared levered out of his chair and turned again to the window. "Well, I *will* be damned. The lone wolf's been ripped to shreds by a she-wolf," he said in disbelief. "Was she worth it?"

Not even a deaf man would have missed the vulgar note in Mack's voice. His crude references to women had always annoyed Jared, but now he was talking about Leza. Suddenly he knew he couldn't tolerate that sort of remark, even if his own thoughts about her had at times been anything but kind.

"My private life's none of your business," Jared said evenly.

"Hey, old buddy—"

"And don't 'old buddy' me. I'm in no mood for it."

"You haven't been in the mood for much of anything lately." Mack snatched up the folder, flopped into the chair in front of Jared's desk, and lapsed into a sullen silence.

Jared, relieved that Mack had dropped the subject without going into his usual Now-is-that-any-way-to-talk-to-the-man-who-saved-your-life routine, took his seat behind his desk and motioned for the folder. With their anger apparently abated, Mack smiled cockily and tossed it to him.

"Jared, I'm sorry to interrupt, but it's important." Neither man had noticed Jared's secretary enter the office. "Mrs. Tyler from the Historical Society just called."

Jared held up one hand. "If this is bad news, Lis, I don't want to hear it."

Twenty-nine, attractive, and strictly business, Lisbeth Daniels had been Jared's secretary for more than six years. He trusted her implicitly and knew that if it had been something minor, she'd have handled it herself.

"Go ahead, let me have it," he relented with a weary sigh.

"The Dixieland project's hit another snag." She eased past Mack to stand next to Jared. "The restoration architect has been called back to Boston. Her mother's suffered a severe stroke."

Jared could only shake his head in frustration. This couldn't be happening again. Only last week the electrician had quit without giving notice, leaving his work half done. A realist at heart, Jared had known from the start that the Dixieland restoration would have its share of problems, but the damned thing had caused more trouble than Sentell Enterprises and Summerset Ranch combined.

Who would have thought that his original idea of purchasing the old Dixieland Hotel and its adjoining twelve acres could have turned into such a nightmare? His problems, as he recalled, had begun the day Mrs. Tyler had gotten wind of his plans to demolish the once renowned, but now dilapidated, three-story building in order to construct a new complex of offices.

"It is your civic duty as a leader in the community," she'd reminded him on more than one occasion, "to help preserve this colorful part of Rosemont's heritage." Never one to be pushed around, Jared had nonetheless been swayed by her pleas to save one of the town's few remaining structures of historical value. Besides, he had reasoned, there were plenty of other choice locations for his complex. How Mrs. Tyler and her Preserve Old Town Committee had persuaded him to restore that old hotel he wasn't sure, but he'd given his word, and now he would see it through to the bitter end.

Lis interrupted his thoughts by handing him several slips of paper. "She asked if you could meet with her and the committee to discuss finding someone to finish the job."

"Can I?" Jared asked, flipping through his messages.

"As a matter of fact," Lis answered, passing him the file labeled *Dixieland Hotel Restoration Project*, "you can."

"Where and when?" Jared picked up his pen to make notes.

"Boardroom at the mall, nine-thirty this morning."

"Remind me to give you a raise."

"You'll have a memo this afternoon." Lis smiled over her shoulder as she made her way toward her own spacious outer office. She stopped abruptly when she encountered Mack blocking her path. His gaze lazily traveled the length of her before coming to rest on her breasts.

"How about lunch?" he asked, finally having the decency to raise his gaze to hers. "I know this intimate little place that serves the best Italian—"

"I have other plans." Lis didn't let him finish his invitation. "I almost forgot," she said, turning to Jared. "She asked me to remind you about escorting her daughter-in-law to the coronation tonight." She laughed when Jared put his face in his hands. He'd forgotten all about that silly Rose Queen thing. He looked up to see Mack on his way out the door behind Lis.

"Can't you take a hint?" Jared said, stopping Mack in his tracks. "She doesn't want to go out with you."

"Women don't know what they want. It's up to us men to keep them straight." He said it with that school-boy grin most people found so charming, but Jared couldn't help noticing that the humor never reached his eyes. "For what it's worth, friend, I hope you work it out with your lady." Before there was time to respond, Mack was out the door, leaving Jared more than a little perplexed.

Just when he thought he had a handle on Mack, he'd do or say something unexpected—such as host a local telethon for abused children or offer a word of comfort to someone, even if they didn't want it. Yes, indeed, Mack was an enigma, but apparently he read Jared like a book. If anyone else had noticed how distracted he'd been of late, they hadn't mentioned it. And distracted he'd been—from the minute he returned home to find Leza and her belongings gone.

Convinced that she must have been half out of her mind from reliving the trauma of the rape, Jared searched frantically for her that first week. He almost started to believe that Leza St. Clair had vanished from the face of the earth. Then Brad mentioned that her vehicle registration had expired. Her personalized license plate and Jake's help made the rest easy. Within a few hours, he knew her address, her phone number—and that she was now Leza Colletti.

Unwilling to believe that fate could be so cruel a third time, Jared had to know more before confronting her. In time, he learned where she worked and that Leza and Steven Colletti had an apartment near the Medical Center, where Colletti was a physical therapist. That's when all the pieces had fallen into place.

He'll find out if I stay! Jared could still hear the panic in Leza's voice when she realized she was in the hospital where Colletti, the man who was now her husband, worked. He'd wrestled with himself about approaching her, but hadn't been certain that he wanted to see her face-to-face when she belonged to another man.

Jared briskly rubbed the tightness in his neck. How had he been so blind? *That* had been her reason for begging him not to leave her there and agreeing to stay on at Summerset. Not just because she needed to recuperate. Not just because later she'd come to care for him. But because she hadn't wanted Steven Colletti to learn that she'd been raped.

Abruptly, he swiveled his chair to stare out the window once again in brooding silence. The anger had long passed. All that was left was the gut-wrenching tightness in his solar plexus, that had become part of his every waking moment.

How had he let this happen again? It had taken him years to come to terms with his past, and for the most part, he had succeeded. He'd finally come to realize that he'd had no control over his mother's desertion. He had been a little boy who loved without question and was hurt without understanding. Now that the years had diminished the pain of losing Marianne, he even understood her reasons for breaking off their relationship. Beautiful, pampered, and self-centered, she never could have adjusted to marriage to a cripple. In a town the size of Rosemont, it was a good thing that he was at least able to put the past behind him. Since Marianne seemed to be involved in every project the town undertook, they were constantly thrown into each other's path.

But he had no one but himself to blame for what had happened with Leza. It had been a most revealing six months. He hadn't realized it before, but unconsciously he had been searching for something, for someone, to fill the emptiness inside him.

Then, as if on cue, enter Leza St. Clair. Hurt and

alone, or so it had seemed, she had come into his life at a time when he desperately needed to be needed, wanted to be wanted. No wonder he had deluded himself into thinking that since she was vulnerable, she was also harmless.

What a joke, he scoffed to himself. He had learned the hard way that Leza St. Clair Colletti was anything but harmless. She was manipulative and conniving, and had selfishly used him. First by playing on his emotions, his need to help her, and then—and this was what rankled most—by making love with him before moving on to Colletti.

If I stop now, I'll never know. The words she'd whispered while in his arms cut through him like a knife. If all she'd wanted was to test her responses to a physical relationship, he thought cynically, he most probably would have obliged. What he resented was her playacting—the false emotions, the pretense of involvement when all she wanted was an experimental roll in the hay. He'd been fooled by the feelings she brought out in him. He'd be more careful in the future.

Something deep inside of him twisted. He didn't want to believe any of it, but his wounded pride and the memories of his mother and Marianne *made* him. For a flicker of a moment, as the pain and anger swelled within him, he wanted to strike back, hurt as he'd been hurt.

Leza's morning had started off well enough. Her alarm had gone off on time for a change, she'd finally tracked down her one pair of run-less pantyhose, and Red had started on the fifth try. She should have known it was too good to be true. Sure enough, things had gone steadily downhill since she'd arrived at work. Two of her six-man crew of display dressers had called in sick, and now she was faced with a practical joker.

"I don't intend to make a federal case out of this," she said, trying to mask her exasperation. "But what if Marcrumb had found this instead of me?" She jerked her thumb over her shoulder at the mannequin everyone affectionately called Waldo the Magnificent. The very obvious, very suggestive bulge behind the zipper of his very expensive designer slacks had been impossible to miss. It was going to be a very long day.

Ignoring the tittering behind her, Leza fished the pair of loosely rolled socks from Waldo's crotch and turned to eye her co-workers. Any other time she might have seen the humor in such a prank, but she was on deadline. Early fall, with the Rose Cavalcade was bearable. But it, and Halloween, were merely preludes to the hectic holiday season that came close on their heels. She simply couldn't spare the time or the energy to run interference between her immediate superior and this imaginative crew.

The foursome suddenly sobered when Leza turned to level a glare at them. Under her scrutiny, their amusement faded to sheepish glances up and down the deserted aisles of the menswear department. Even if it took all morning, she vowed, she would find out who was intent on making her life miserable today.

The smirk that flitted across Bob Weber's face was a dead giveaway. She wasn't surprised. The man had been nothing but a thorn in her side from her first day at Randolph's. He had been Keith Cathcart's assistant, and it was common knowledge that he had fully expected to be the new Director of Visual Merchandising when Cathcart transferred to the Shreveport store. Leza, normally sympathetic to a fault, could understand Weber's resentment, but his petty attempts at sabotage had to stop.

She squared her shoulders and locked her gaze with

Weber's. His smile withered instantly. Before she had time to feel any real satisfaction, though, the display at his back caught her attention. The lump inside the tiger-stripped bikini briefs made Waldo's look positively respectable. Silently, she counted to ten as she brushed past Weber to retrieve what she suspected was yet another pair of socks.

The mannequin, a limbless torso model, sat perched high atop a pedestal display, forcing Leza on tiptoe as she fumbled with the elastic waistband.

"Hello, Leza."

Leza froze in place. It had been six long months, but she would have recognized that voice anywhere. Her heart actually skipped a beat, and it took every ounce of willpower she had to turn and face the man she had both dreaded and dreamed of seeing again.

He looked the same, a little tired perhaps, but wonderful nonetheless. At first his eyes glinted like steel, hard and unyielding, with something akin to hostility making her want to put some distance between them. No sooner did she notice it when the hardness disappeared to be replaced by a glimmer of . . . what? Amusement? She followed his gaze and suddenly felt like a kid caught with her hand in the cookie jar—or, in this case, with her hand inside a man's pants.

She jerked her hand free with such force that the mannequin wobbled precariously and would have toppled over on her if Jared hadn't pulled her out of harm's way—and into his arms. The mannequin hit the floor with a loud clatter, but all Leza heard was her heart hammering wildly inside her breast.

Jared looked down, all humor gone from his expression. "I seem to make a habit of rescuing you." His voice held a rugged, seductive edge. His hands burned through her sweater, resurrecting memories of more intimate caresses.

Pull away, she told herself, but her legs refused to cooperate. His fingers tightened, almost painfully, triggering a warning bell inside her head. Alarmed, she glanced up to see that the hardness had returned to rob those wonderful gray eyes of all warmth. Why was he so angry when, if she remembered correctly, she was the one who had been slighted? The silence would have gone on forever if Leza's assistant hadn't spoken up.

"Are you all right?" Peggy asked, glancing from Leza to Jared. To anyone else it might have sounded as though she were asking about the near accident with the mannequin, but Leza knew better.

A petite, blue-eyed blonde, Peggy Johnson was more than Leza's assistant. In the short time they'd known each other, she had become a friend and confidante. She had proven her loyalty by backing Leza's ideas about the reorganization of the display department, which had been sadly outdated and in desperate need of a fresh, new perspective. Leza saw the determined set to Peggy's jaw, the willful look in her eyes. She was there to help Leza in any way she could—even if it meant coming up against someone as imposing as Jared Sentell.

Leza quickly extricated herself from Jared's grasp. "Yes, of course," she assured her friend. "No harm done."

The quiet of the pre-business hours hung in the air, amplifying every sound, every movement. Jared's unexpected appearance had momentarily unbalanced Leza, exposing a vulnerability she had striven to conceal. In her first few months at Randolph's, it had been difficult to gain the respect due her title. With the exception of Bob Weber, she had succeeded in winning everyone's acceptance as an equal, not just another woman out to do a man's job. Now, looking at the curious faces around her, Leza feared that all had been lost. It unnerved her that Jared's presence could so completely undo everything she'd worked so hard to accomplish.

Unwittingly, Bob Weber came to the rescue when the smirk Leza had learned to recognize as a portent of trouble once more crept across his face. She stiffened her backbone and took charge like the professional she knew she was.

"Peggy, you and Judy get started on the jewelry display. Mr. Gordon's approved all my changes. Larry and Bob, take down the scaffold in housewares and I'll let you know what to do next." She watched them scatter and wondered why it was so easy to be in control at work when her personal life always seemed to be in a turmoil.

Within seconds, she was alone with Jared. His rigid stance made her so uncomfortable that it was all she could do to keep from turning on her heels and following her workers. As if he sensed her thoughts, Jared seized her roughly at the elbow and led her to an out-of-the-way alcove.

"Don't look so scared, Leza. I'm not here to let any skeletons out of that closet of yours," he said, so harshly that Leza literally fell back a step. "Or to drag you back to my bed."

She felt the color draining from her face and would have slapped him if she hadn't been so shocked.

"You're hurting me," she returned through clenched teeth, jerking free when he loosened his grip. She tried to leave, but he stepped into her path.

"Don't run out on me again," he warned, his features tight, frightening.

"Don't bully me, Jared," she returned his warning. *Please don't do this to me*, she pleaded silently, relieved when his features softened.

"We have to talk." He said it so quietly that she had to strain to hear. Then, with more emphasis, he added, "We're going to talk. We can do it here, or we can do it on neutral ground over lunch."

Angered again by his brusque behavior, Leza tried to sidestep him. Still, he barred her path. She glanced up, her heart pounding. "Not today," she told him as succinctly as the trembling that threatened to explode inside her allowed. "I have too much work—"

"Today." His stance, his tone, his expression all said that he would brook no argument.

"Mr. Sentell."

Jared and Leza both whirled around at the unexpected voice. Neither had seen Paul Marcrumb approaching.

"I see Mrs. Tyler got in touch with you. Glad you could make it on such short notice." Marcrumb pumped Jared's arm in a vigorous handshake. "I was just on my way to the boardroom. I'll walk with you, if you're ready." He looked from Jared to Leza, his dark eyes speculative.

"I'll be right with you, Paul," Jared acknowledged Marcrumb's offer before turning his attention back to Leza. "Lunch at twelve. I'll find you." Before Leza could protest, Jared was engrossed in conversation with her boss.

Several seconds passed before she was able to pull her thoughts together. When she did, she was amazed by the amount of detail she noticed in that short time. Both men were tall and well built; both were impeccably dressed. But Paul Marcrumb, an attractive man in his own right, paled in comparison to Jared. Leza knew at that very moment that even if she never saw Jared again, she would never forget the way he moved, the seductive way he had of speaking to her, the gentleness of his touch.

But where, she wondered, had that gentleness been

today? He'd looked at her with such hostility that it had frightened her. So much, in fact, that all she wanted was to to get away. She only hoped that her shaking legs would support her long enough to make it to the privacy of her office.

Taking the escalator to the third floor where all the offices were located, she made her way down the long, narrow corridor to her own small workshop. Without turning on the light, she crossed the cluttered room to literally collapse on the sofa.

Protected by the darkness, the tears began to fall— the only ones she'd given in to since that first lonely night away from Summerset. All it had taken to open the floodgates had been seeing Jared for less than two minutes. For the first time in months, she was filled with doubt about herself. Emotionally drained, Leza stretched out on the sofa.

Had she been lying to herself all this time, believing that she had grown strong enough to live each day to the fullest? No, damn it! She *was* stronger, better. The therapy sessions, she knew, had worked wonders. She had regained her sense of self-worth. She no longer avoided contact with strangers. She was especially proud that she had finally worked out all her hangups resulting from the rape, the worst being her fear that the rapist might one day pop back into her life. Nothing, she realized now, had prepared her for this encounter with Jared.

During her first few days in Rosemont, she lived on tenterhooks, fearful that Jared might be looking for her, that she might accidentally run into him. As the days turned into weeks, and the weeks into months, she nurtured that last image of Jared on horseback: his icy, impersonal look as he tipped his hat as he would to any stranger before he turned and rode away. That memory never failed to remind her of why she had run away without a word. She would not impose herself on a man who was obviously having second thoughts about his involvement with her.

We're going to talk, he'd said. About what? Hadn't the look he'd thrown her that last morning said it all? Wasn't it evident in the way he'd just treated her that her dreams about being with him again had been just that—dreams? In despair, she laid her forearm across her eyes and tried to blot out the look on his face. She didn't hear the door open, didn't realize that she wasn't alone until Peggy spoke.

"Are you all right?" The bright stream of light from the open doorway filled the tiny office. Quickly wiping away the tears streaming down her cheeks, Leza forced herself into a sitting position.

"I'm fine, Peggy." Leza was thankful that her voice, although weak, was steady, but she was finding it hard to ignore the pain in her head.

"Why are you sitting in the dark?" Peggy asked, reaching for the light switch.

"Please don't," Leza said, this time hearing the quaver in her voice. "I have a terrible headache," she explained, quickly rummaging through her purse for the aspirin bottle. She took two tablets and downed them with a sip of the soft drink she'd left on her desk earlier.

Peggy left the door slightly ajar and took a seat next to Leza. "Heartache is more like it," she said, brushing Leza's hair behind one ear. "My word, Leza, you look awful."

"Thanks, I needed that." Leza's attempt to lighten the mood went unrewarded when Peggy leaned forward to pierce her with a look.

"I'm a good listener, boss. Want to tell me about him?"

In the months they had known each other, they'd shared secrets and dreams, even a frustration or two, but there were two things Leza simply had not been able to share with anyone, not Peggy, not even Steven: the rape and her involvement with Jared.

"There's nothing to tell, Peggy. Jared is just someone I haven't seen in a very long time."

"Just someone isn't exactly how I'd describe that one," Peggy's pale-blue eyes positively gleamed. "He's just about the most gorgeous man I've ever laid eyes on."

Leza smiled. "Steven's going to love hearing that," she teased, waiting for the flush of color that would soon cover Peggy's fair complexion. The mention of Leza's brother never failed to leave Peggy ever so slightly flustered.

"Go ahead," Peggy countered, surprising Leza with her words, but not disappointing her when her face turned the most fetching shade of pink. "Just because Steve's my one and only, doesn't mean I've gone blind."

It was difficult to show any real appreciation for Peggy's remark when all Leza could think of were smouldering gray eyes and one rakish dimple. Wearily, she closed her eyes and rested her head on the back of the sofa.

"Why don't you go home and rest up for the coronation tonight?" Peggy offered with a gentle pat on Leza's hand. "You obviously aren't up to working today. I'll handle things here."

Leza sighed and forced one eye open. "That is tonight, isn't it?" How could she give the crowning of the Rose Queen her complete and undivided attention when all she wanted was to find a nice, quiet place to be alone?

"Thanks, but I can't do that. Weber would just love it if I didn't get the Halloween displays up until after Thanksgiving."

Peggy feigned a look of hurt. "Hey, don't you think I'm capable of hanging orange and black crepe paper and dressing a couple of mannequins in goblin garb?" she asked indignantly. "And don't worry about Weber. I was handling him long before you came to Randolph's, remember?"

It still amazed Leza that there was no rivalry, no animosity between the two of them. After all, Peggy had been here almost as long as Weber, who never missed an opportunity to remind everyone that if Randolph's had had its quota of female executives, he'd have her job. The accusation was, of course, absurd, but without it he would have to accept that Leza was not only better qualified for the position, but doing an excellent job. It was simply the only way he had of soothing his wounded male ego.

"Go on home," Peggy said. "I'll take care of everything here. It's not like you don't have it all under control. Besides, it's emergencies like this that should make you grateful for having such a good, competent assistant."

The pain in Leza's head had grown steadily worse while they talked, shooting up from her neck into the base of her skull. If she could just relax for awhile, she could cope with everything better. She knew she'd be no good tonight if she didn't get rid of this headache.

"You talked me into it," she said, gathering her coat and purse. "Call me if—"

"Just get out of here before I change my mind," Peggy scolded, motioning Leza toward the door and answering the telephone at the same time.

Outside her office, Leza paused in the hallway. The escalator was closer, but the freight elevator, she decided, was much safer. She didn't want to risk running into anyone and having to explain why she was leaving.

Especially Jared.

TEN

Leza let herself in and dead-bolted the door before hanging her coat in the hall closet. The aspirin hadn't yet taken effect. From past experience, she knew the only thing that might possibly help would be a nice long nap.

Facing the room, she let her gaze sweep the bright, airy apartment she'd shared with Steven for the past six months. Typically modern, it had never been particularly to her liking. But today, even with all its chrome and glass and splashes of wild color highlighting the varying shades of gray and white, it was her haven.

She stepped down into the sunken den and angled toward the long, slate-colored sofa facing the stone fireplace that dominated one entire wall.

Suddenly, she longed for her own furnishings, her own bric-a-brac, her own space. So far, her arrangement with Steven had worked out nicely. They shared everything from the housework and expenses to the shopping chores. She had to admit, too, that he had been wonderful about Hoover, whose curiosity about

Steven's pride and joy, an eight-foot aquarium, had to be constantly monitored. He had even encouraged her to add her own homey touches—a fern here, a fluffy pillow there—but still, it wasn't the same. It was his apartment, his kitchen, his spare bedroom with the king-size waterbed and mirrors on the ceiling.

Exhausted, Leza kicked off her shoes and stretched out on the sofa. Her arms, when she raised them to rub her throbbing temples, felt heavy. Maybe if she just closed her eyes for a few minutes . . .

She was neither asleep nor awake, and little by little she began to lose all sense of the present. At first, she tried to suppress the images that grew stronger with each passing second. She knew where they were leading, but she was simply too tired to fight them this time . . . Leza curled into a tight, fetal ball and allowed the past to gradually take control.

It started coming back slowly in the beginning: the days with her family before leaving Odessa; all her preparations for the long drive that would be her first step on the road to her new life; her many stops along the way. But then the memories came faster, like a slide show she couldn't control. Small towns that had been only names on a Texas map—Iraan, Ozona, Sonora, San Marcos—all became points of interest to explore at her leisure as she traveled southward toward San Antonio, then back up to Austin and Lake Travis. From there, she headed to Waco, where she decided to shorten her trip and cut across to Athens, and finally to Canton to spend the afternoon at the town's renowned First Monday Trade Days.

Knowing that Rosemont was less than an hour's drive away, she hadn't pressed herself. There had been so much to see and do, so many booths filled with arts and crafts and antiques to be perused that time had completely gotten away from her. It was almost dark by the time she left the bustling little community with her one and only purchase—a scrawny, flea-ridden, calico kitten.

Roughly ten more miles, she remembered thinking, and she'd be on Steven's doorstep, surprising him by arriving a full two weeks earlier than expected. It was then that Red had coughed, sputtered, and finally died—forcing her to coast into a deserted roadside park.

This wasn't the first time Red had conked out on her, and she was reminded once again of her father's warning when she had told him of her decision to buy a car on her own. She'd wanted something sleek and sporty, unlike the station wagon Don had insisted she drive, but prices had sent her searching for a good, used bargain. The eight-year-old Corvette captured both her heart and her price range, and, over her father's objections, she made a small down payment and agreed to pay for it in monthly installments. A year later, her last payment and her vehicle's registration had come due at the same time. Doing something completely out of character, she splurged and ordered a personalized license plate number—*Paid 4*.

Her father had been right, as usual. Red had been nothing but one headache, one repair bill after another. If only she hadn't been so bent on doing things by herself, her father would have co-signed a loan for a new car and she wouldn't be in this predicament now.

Never one to dwell on if-only's, Leza gingerly raised the hood in hopes of finding something obvious—a loose wire, a broken belt, something minor that she could repair by herself. But her only luck, she realized, had been in coming to a stop under the one working street lamp in the park.

Nervously, she began to pace back and forth. What was she to do now? She glanced back at Red parked in the shadows behind her. With its hood gaping open, it reminded her of a hungry nestling demanding to be fed. No matter how childish it might have been, Leza resented the cantankerous vehicle having the nerve to look as if it was demanding anything.

In the distance, two tiny streaks of light sliced through the darkness, moving steadily toward her down the lonely stretch of Texas Highway 64. She watched the lights grow brighter and closer. Soon she could hear boisterous voices and laughter floating through the humid night air. Then, as the glare of a pickup's headlights bounced off her in passing, illuminating her solitary figure, the first prickle of anxiety swept over her. She wrapped her arms around herself, not for added warmth, because the spring night was sultry and warm, but to help still the trembling that threatened to steal over her.

"Hey, Brad, back it up!" an excited male voice rang out. Other voices chimed in, loud and crude in their enthusiasm. The truck screeched to a halt, then backed up, slinging dirt and gravel in its wake.

Anxiety turned quickly to dread when Leza saw four young men in the back of the truck. They all stood and, stumbling from side to side, tried to orient themselves to the sudden stop. Three others craned their necks from inside the cab to ogle her. Then there was nothing but quiet as one tall, barrel-chested youth managed to stagger down the length of the cargo bed. Several seconds ticked by as he swayed, giving Leza the impression that he was trying to focus on her.

"Say, lady, ya look like ya could use a man 'bout now," he said at long last.

Leza recognized the voice as the one that had called out earlier. Only now that it was closer and not distorted by the wind, she also recognized a distinct drunken slur. Foreboding overtook her and was manifested by gooseflesh. She prayed fervently that drunks couldn't smell fear like dogs. She knew instantly that she couldn't let them know they had rattled her. They were probably harmless enough, but alcohol had a way of making even the most harmless man a potential threat. Any show of fear could be her downfall.

Calmly addressing the only one of them who was capable of doing more than staring dumbly down at her, Leza looked directly into eyes she suspected were not only dark brown, but bloodshot as well.

"Thanks, but my brother's on his way," she lied with the hope that the mere mention of a man would dampen their alcohol-inflated bravado. She didn't miss the glances that passed among them when a shorter, less strongly built boy ambled toward the rear of the truck.

"She's lyin', Evan. Ain't nobody coming out here." None too gently, he nudged the boy he'd called Evan, almost knocking him to the ground. A string of curses and a clumsy grappling match ensued, with Evan juggling a can of beer in his right hand. Righting himself, he up-ended the can while the others urged him on with hoots of approval as he chugged down the brew. Obviously pleased with his accomplishment, he grinned and dragged the furry length of his forearm across his lips.

"I know that," he said through a belch, and threw one muscular leg over the tailgate. "I'm drunk, not stupid."

"C'mon, Evan. Leave her alone," someone called from inside the truck.

"What's the matter, Brad, you scared your daddy's gonna throw us all in his jail?" The smirk that crept across Evan's face was probably meant to be macho, but it didn't quite make it. Instead, it just made him look silly. No sooner had he thrown his other leg over the tailgate to climb down, than a blinding glare of headlights stopped him in his tracks.

"Are these boys bothering you, Miss?"

Things seemed to slip into fast-forward from that

point on: Seven pairs of eyes jerked toward the sound of the deep, authoritative voice. Behind Leza, a door opened and then slammed shut, immediately jolting the driver of the pickup into reckless action. Again dirt and gravel flew.

Thrown completely off balance by the fishtailing motion, the boys standing in the back of the truck went sprawling on top of each other. It was a comical sight, made even more so by their high-pitched cries, which competed with the squeal of the tires until the pickup disappeared in the distance.

"Are you all right?"

Forgetting momentarily that she wasn't alone, Leza turned abruptly, and almost collided with the man who had sent the rowdy bunch packing. The headlights from his car bathed them both in light. Glancing up, Leza all but caught her breath at the soft brown eyes studying her. A tall man of medium build, he was dressed in dark, form-fitting dress slacks and a crisply starched white shirt that stood out in stark relief against his tan. He looked to be in his mid- to late-thirties and, as far as appearances went, he was probably the closest thing to perfection she'd ever seen. She had no trouble picturing him stepping right out of the pages of *Gentleman's Quarterly*. He made her feel dowdy in comparison.

"Yes, thanks to you, Mr . . . ?"

"Maxwell," he said, extending his right hand. "Tom Maxwell, Miss . . . ?" he turned the question back to her. His gaze seemed to take in every detail of her in one quick movement.

"I'm Leza Colletti and, again, thank you." She took his hand, but when she tried to break the contact, his grip tightened ever so slightly. Under normal circumstances, she might have regarded the gesture as the prelude to a harmless flirtation, but she was still shaken by her encounter with seven inebriated youngsters. All she felt now was threatened.

Forcing a nervous laugh, she gently but firmly tugged her hand free. "That was the funniest thing I've ever seen," she said, noting that he was probably five or six inches taller than herself. It made her uncomfortable that he stood too close, and that his eyes never left her face. She took a few steps backward to put some distance between them. "It was like watching the Three Stooges, Laurel and Hardy, and Abbott and Costello all in the same movie."

The smile on his too-perfect face faded, but not before she noticed that as charming as it had been, there was something about it that made her uneasy. She couldn't put her finger on it, but it was enough for her to resolve to keep her distance.

"I'm glad you see the humor in it," he said. She forced herself not to look away when his eyes darkened to the deepest shade of brown she'd ever seen. Surely it was just her nerves playing tricks on her. No one could look that good and that ominous at the same time.

"You're right, of course," she said, surprised at how close her words came to being an apology. "I suppose I'm just trying to find something to laugh at so I won't cry. There's no telling what would have happened if you hadn't shown up when you did."

"Come now, Miss Colletti. We're both adults and know exactly what they had on their minds." Again, Leza sensed something threatening in those soft, brown eyes and heard a hint of something less than congenial in his voice. Before there was time to fully ponder it, his friendly smile returned. This time it was punctuated with one deep dimple in each cheek.

"But let's not think of unpleasant things," he said, gently brushing past her to stand in front of Red. "I take it you've had car trouble. Let's see what I can do.'' He worked the knot from his tie, rolled up his sleeves, then ducked his head beneath the hood.

Relieved that he had turned his attention elsewhere, Leza watched him examine each belt, each wire that she'd checked earlier. What bothered her more than anything was that she had allowed her imagination to run wild. But, she defended herself, what woman wouldn't be wary finding herself stranded and alone miles from nowhere?

A sudden frenzy of movement inside the car reminded her that they weren't exactly alone. Obviously bored, the calico kitten she'd resorted to calling Cat—for no other reason than not having had time to come up with a decent name—skittered along the dashboard, tried to wrap itself around the steering wheel, then leaped for the headrest on the driver's seat. Amused, Leza picked up Cat and stroked her head until she finally nestled contentedly against her breast.

Tom Maxwell worked in silence for several minutes, then straightened up and pulled a handkerchief from his hip pocket. He looked heavenward when a few isolated raindrops fell from the sky.

''Oh, great,'' Leza muttered. ''Just what I need.''

''I have to agree.'' He smiled and chuckled, and it was the most pleasant sound she'd heard all evening. She smiled back in spite of herself. ''If it wasn't for bad luck, you'd have no luck at all tonight. With the exception of meeting me, of course.'' There it was again, that little-boy smile that almost made her forget her misgivings about him. He folded the dirtied handkerchief neatly, then stuffed it back into his pants pocket. ''I'm afraid the problem's just a bit more than this shade-tree mechanic can handle. It'll have to be towed to town tomorrow. I know a good mechanic who works cheap.'' The streetlight glowed softly, shimmering on the thatch of gold-brown hair that fell across his forehead. "I'll give you a ride, if you're headed into town."

"I just don't know," she hedged, still refusing to ignore her woman's intuition.

As though he sensed her reluctance, he leaned against Red's fender. "You're right to be cautious, Miss Colletti, but I can't in good conscience leave you stranded with a thunderstorm brewing and a truck load of boozed-up teenagers on the prowl." He straightened up and looked directly at her. "I sure wouldn't want someone to just drive away and leave my wife alone like this." Another volley of raindrops pelted them, raising the pungent odor of heat, rain, and road dust. And something else, a scent so pleasant, so familiar that Leza instinctively closed her eyes and breathed in the tobacco-y aroma that had always clung to her father. "And think about it. If you do decide to spend the night in your car, you'll still be faced with the problem of having it repaired in the morning." He showed his first sign of annoyance when she hesitated.

"Look, if it'll make you feel better, I have a friend who lives just off the main road. You can use his phone to let someone know what's happened."

Caution had to be her first concern, but she also had to be logical. Since she hadn't talked with Steven since her spur-of-the-moment decision to cut her vacation short, he had no idea she was within two-hundred miles of Rosemont, much less just outside the city limits. She couldn't backtrack to find a telephone because there had been no houses or service stations along the way. Only the unknown lay ahead. Home was over four-hundred miles behind her. Suddenly it was crystal clear that by exercising her prerogatives as a liberated woman, she had, unfortunately, gotten herself into a predicament.

And to make matters worse, Tom Maxwell was right about spending the night alone on the side of the road.

Even without the threat of the gang of boys returning, the prospect of sleeping in a bucket seat all night held little appeal for her.

Still, her earlier instincts niggled at her.

She glanced down the desolate stretch of highway that ran east and west like a giant ribbon of black. In the distance, lightning illuminated the night again and again, creating an eerie backdrop for the dense forest that lined each side of the road. Thunder rumbled a warning, but not soon enough to keep them from getting drenched when the clouds opened and rain fell in buckets.

Leza hugged the kitten protectively against her body and called above the wind that seemed to have come from nowhere, "It doesn't take a ton of bricks—"

"No," Maxwell interrupted, quickly propelling her toward his sleek, silver Town Car. "Just gallons of water. Get settled while I secure your car."

Minutes later, he slid behind the wheel and handed her her keys and handbag. "Just in the nick of time." He threw her another breathtaking smile and pulled onto the road.

The sight of a pipe nestled in the ashtray put a smile on Leza's lips. She leaned back, enjoying the new-car smell mingling with the spicy aroma that again reminded her of home. Even Cat, who had spooked when the rain started, calmed down and curled up in Leza's lap. In a matter of seconds, the kitten was soundly asleep.

All these things—the fragrant odors, the purring kitten, the gentle whirring of the air conditioner as it efficiently removed the stifling humid air—lulled Leza into a sense of security so complete that she didn't question him when they turned onto a small, red clay road. He had, after all, mentioned that his friend lived just off the main road.

They rode in silence for a mile or so and Leza didn't immediately recognize the uneasy feeling that had gradually crept over her. But suddenly she knew that something was wrong, terribly wrong. She felt it as surely as the coolness of the air conditioner on her damp skin.

As she chanced a guarded glance to her left, she heard quiet laughter and one word so softly spoken that she wasn't sure she'd heard it at all.

"Easy," he said, but Leza had the impression that he wasn't speaking to her.

Tom Maxwell sat straight and rigid, arms extended with both hands draped over the steering wheel at the wrists. The light from the instrument panel glowed green and ghostly on his face. The same features she'd found so appealing just moments ago were now hard and unyielding in profile.

The fine hair on the back of Leza's neck rose and gooseflesh covered her. She had heard the expression horror stricken, but until she saw his hand leave the steering wheel and press the button on the console that locked both doors, she had only associated it with scary movies and Steven King novels.

Again he chuckled, this time louder and longer, and when he turned toward Leza, a lump rose in her throat. As suddenly as the laughter had started, it died. He leveled a glare at her so full of contempt that she shrank against the door.

"So goddamn easy." No longer was he her congenial rescuer, the beautiful man with the little-boy charm. Here was the devil himself.

She had thought the most evil thing she'd ever heard had been his laughter just seconds earlier. She had been wrong. This time when he spoke, his voice filled her with terror.

"Works every time . . ."

* * *

Soaked with perspiration, Leza came back to the present with a start when something thudded softly beside her on the sofa. Several seconds passed while she waited for the trembling to subside and the nausea to pass. Hoover nuzzled her neck. Then, purring, waited for the favor to be returned.

Grateful to be pulled away from her dark dream, Leza rolled onto her back and snuggled the pet closer for comfort. It took a little doing, but at last she willed her pulse rate back to normal.

The dreams, the recall, had grown less frequent over the months. But when they crept up on her as they had just now, they were every bit as vivid and terrifying as that night so long ago. God, how she prayed that it wouldn't always be that way.

Hoover, who stayed in a perpetual state of friskiness, pranced down the length of her torso. Leza couldn't help smiling.

"I see Steven forgot to put the lid on the sugar bowl again," she said, brushing away the telltale particles of white that clung to the pesky feline's whiskers. Huge green eyes blinked at her unashamedly before being drawn toward the gurgling of the fish tank. At times like this, she was grateful for the distraction of Hoover's antics.

"Oh, no you don't." Leza sat up and made Hoover look her square in the eyes. "He'll forgive almost anything, but not tormenting his angels. Now, scoot," she scolded, releasing Hoover and laughing when the cat shot down the hall in search of another adventure.

Leza glanced at her watch and winced. Twelve-fifteen. She'd closed her eyes for only a few minutes, it seemed, but almost three hours had passed since she'd left Randolph's. Thankfully, the pain in her head was gone. And she'd grown adept at pulling herself together after the bad dreams. There was still time to get back to work, and maybe before anyone other than Peggy knew she had left. She'd just freshen her makeup and be on her way.

The mirror in the bathroom told a woeful tale. Not only was her makeup a mess, but her clothes looked as though she'd slept in them, which, of course, she had. She was just tossing her sweater and tan linen skirt into the hamper when the doorbell rang insistently—once, twice, then again and again.

Steven, she thought, remembering that it was his turn to do the grocery shopping. And because it was his regular bowling night, he must have decided to save time by shopping on his lunch break. Then, seeing her car in the carport, she reasoned, he probably had opted for ringing the bell over fumbling with his own keys.

The only garment in sight was Steven's black velour bathrobe, hanging in its usual place on a hook on the back of the bathroom door. Quickly slipping into it, she raced down the hall.

"Hold your horses," she called, reaching the door and flinging it open.

Her first impulse was to slam the door in Jared's face. Her second was to slap his hand away when he braced the door open with one strong hand.

"What are you doing here?" she demanded, forcing an icy edge to her voice. He tried to close the door behind him, but Leza quickly pushed it all the way open. If he insisted on barging in on her, she wanted at least one small advantage.

"Have it your way," he said, sauntering past her into the living room. She followed him as far as the step-down.

"Jared, this isn't a good time."

His back was to her, and several uncomfortable seconds passed before she saw what captured his attention. On the mantle, centered between four bowling trophies, was a photograph of Steven and herself. It was her favorite, a copy of the one they'd had made for their mother's birthday last month. The photographer, a silly young woman who had flirted outrageously with Steven, posed Leza sitting with Steven standing behind her, one hand resting on her shoulder.

Jared turned abruptly, his eyes flickering over the length of her before locking boldly with hers.

"It's as good a time as any."

In the whole six months, he hadn't once bothered to contact her. Now, out of the blue, he was in her apartment demanding that they talk. He had a lot of nerve.

In a nervous gesture, she tugged the lapels of the oversized robe more snugly together, then tightened the sash. She didn't miss the way his eyes slid over her, or the way his eyebrows pulled together. "Seriously, Jared, I have to get back to work. I have more important—"

Moving more quickly than she thought was humanly possible, Jared closed the distance separating them to grab her roughly by both arms.

"Don't," he said, and she heard the warning in that one word. "Don't tell me you have more important things to do than get things straight between us."

He had never treated her so harshly before. It should should have frightened her. Instead, it made her angry. With a force that shocked them both, she tore loose from his grasp. "And don't you ever manhandle me like that again." Adrenaline coursed through her veins, making her tremble violently.

"What the hell's going on?" Steven stood in the open doorway, a grocery bag in one hand, a six-pack of beer in the other. Leza saw that he instantly read the situation, sensing that she was distressed. Before she could explain, he relieved himself of his burden and placed his six-foot frame between Leza and Jared. The two men glared unflinchingly at each other.

"Stay out of this, Colletti." The threat in Jared's voice was unmistakable. "This is none of your affair."

Leza had known Steven all her life, understood him as well as she understood herself. She thought she'd grown to know Jared during her stay at Summerset, but she didn't understand *this* Jared or his hostility. Before she could blink an eye the two men had sized each other up, and she quickly sandwiched herself between them.

"Steven, please," she pleaded. "It's okay. I'll handle it." Opinionated and overprotective though he might be, Steven had never been one to be too aggressive. She'd seen Steven this angry only once before, when she was ten and Johnny McBride had held her head underwater longer than was playful. No one ever knew exactly what had happened, but Johnny had wound up in the emergency room with a broken nose.

Steven's face remained rigid, his eyes trained on Jared. She had to reach up and touch his face to get his attention. That innocent gesture seemed to unleash something reckless in Jared.

"I just want to know one thing," Jared said, his words directed at Leza, but his eyes still locked with Steven's. "Was sleeping with me just a test run after the rape—"

"No!" Leza heard herself scream. She couldn't believe he would be so cruel. "Jared, please don't."

"Rape?" The word sounded ugly coming from her brother's lips. "What's he talking about, Sis?" He looked as though Jared had landed a physical blow.

From that point on, things became a blur.

Jared's face loomed above her, his expression one of shock, incredulity. "Sis?" she thought she heard him say. Then she felt as if his hands were on her shoulders.

Their words and voices sounded garbled. She screamed Steven's name when he dragged Jared away from her and shoved him up against the wall. Jared retaliated and drew back his fist . . .

Leza was as helpless as someone watching a scene in a movie, unable to stop the action on the big screen. She felt her strength deserting her, her limbs go rubbery. Her only thought was that for the first time in her life she was going to faint. The room began to spin, slant sideways. She thought she saw Jared's lips move, saying her name, just as everything went bright-bright, then faded to cool, blessed blackness.

ELEVEN

Passing out wasn't something Leza ever wanted to do again, but at least Jared was nowhere to be seen when she came to. Steven knelt beside the sofa, applying a cool cloth to her forehead.

"Is he gone?"

Steven nodded solemnly. "We decided it was probably best if he weren't here when you woke up."

She wanted to ask if Jared had left quietly, but Steven didn't give her the chance. "No, he didn't give me a hard time," he answered her unasked question. "The man may be a hothead, but . . ." He paused and appeared to be collecting his thoughts. "But I don't think he meant you any harm." He removed the cloth from her head and briskly rubbed it across each wrist. "Feeling better?"

She still felt a bit faint, but at least the room had stopped spinning. "What about you?" She searched his face for any sign of physical violence. The last thing she remembered was Jared drawing back his fist . . .

"Hey, I'm fine," Steven quickly assured her. "Nary

a blow was landed, unless you count your head hitting the floor." He grinned that lopsided grin that made him look every bit of fourteen again. Leza suddenly wanted, *needed*, to tell her big brother everything that had happened. She'd kept it to herself far too long.

"We need to talk, Sis," Steven voiced her thoughts aloud. "You up to telling me what's going on?"

The words weren't even out yet, and already she knew that it would be a cleansing of the soul to finally get it all out in the open. "Yes," she said, and as calmly as possible began to relate the entire story.

Careful not to dwell on details, she found it easier than she'd thought possible to tell him about the assault, and about her time at Summerset. Surprisingly, she wanted to tell him about her involvement with Jared, including their one night together and that last morning when his cold, impersonal look had broken her heart.

Steven listened without interruption until she stopped talking. Then he gathered her in his arms and held her, held her so tightly that it was hard for her to breathe. At long last, Leza drew back and the tears in his eyes were her undoing. She clung to him, just like she had when Johnny McBride scared her long ago, and just like she had the night Amy died. All this time she had made herself sick worrying about his reaction. She thought he would demand to know all the sordid details, would be angry enough to kill, worried enough to demand that she run home to Mom and Dad. Not once had it occurred to her how hurt he would be.

"All these months you've suffered through this alone," he said. She picked up something else she hadn't expected. He felt guilty.

"Oh, Steven," she was quick to console. "There was nothing you could have done, and I haven't been alone. Where do you think I go every Thursday evening?"

"You said you were working."

"I couldn't very well tell you that I was going to the Women's Crisis Center to meet with my support group, now could I?"

"But it isn't the same. They're strangers."

She took his hand and made him meet her eyes. "Strangers, yes. But strangers with a common bond."

He considered that a moment. Leza soon saw that what she had said satisfied him, consoled him.

"What about Mom and Dad?"

"I don't want them to know, Steven." She was adamant. "What good would it do? As bad as it was, it's over and I'm okay now." Again she forced eye contact. "And if you're this hurt by it, imagine how it would affect them."

It took a few seconds for him to realize that she was right, and then he nodded his agreement. "What about the police. Have they found the son-of-a-bitch?" The gentleness in his voice and facial features was replaced with stony anger.

This was what she'd been dreading. He was over the initial shock, and now his big-brother instincts had kicked in.

Not wanting to look small and vulnerable, to be at any disadvantage, she stood and looked down at him. "I didn't file a report when it happened because I didn't remember anything and it seemed useless. When my memory came back, it was all I could do to deal with something I had never truly wanted to believe had happened in the first place. And now . . ." She stopped and looked down at her hands clutched tightly in front of her. "Well, now it's been so long . . ." Why had it suddenly become so hard to talk to him? "I just don't want to go through it all again. And," she said, raising one perfectly arched eyebrow, "I don't want to discuss it further. I have to get back to work."

"You can't run from it forever, Leza," he called,

stopping her at her bedroom door. She turned to find him sitting exactly where she'd left him. He was one of the strongest men she'd ever known, but he looked absolutely helpless.

"Maybe not," she calmly told him, "but I can try to keep one step ahead of it for as long as I can." She saw that he wanted to say more, but stopped him with an abrupt, "Don't wait up for me tonight. I'll be late."

Keeping track of twelve Rose Queen hopefuls and working around their adoring, often overbearing parents was a bigger job than organizing the entire program had been. Leza was in the middle of rechecking every last-minute detail when she paused to peek through the curtains from backstage.

The rest of the afternoon had been hectic, but not hectic enough to keep her mind from rehashing every event of the day, starting with Jared popping unexpectedly back into her life and ending with her heart-to-heart talk with Steven. She couldn't remember exactly when, but sometime between leaving the apartment and arriving at Tyler Auditorium she made a decision. No matter how well Steven had taken the news, she could no longer live under the same roof with him.

He had been waiting outside her bedroom door when she came out dressed and ready to return to Randolph's. Clearly, he'd had time to collect his thoughts, as well as his wits. According to Steven, the logical thing to do was to report the rape to the authorities. Since she had regained her memory, surely she could tell them something that would help track down the "low-life son of scum" who was probably still on the loose. And, he informed her without the bat of an eyelash, he felt that until they found him, Leza would be safer back in Odessa. Yes, indeed, Big Brother was alive and well and still had all the answers.

All afternoon she fumed over his presumptuous demands. And she didn't think it was possible for anything else to surprise her today.

But then she didn't expect to see Jared escorting Marianne Prescott-Tyler down the center aisle of Tyler Auditorium.

The names Prescott and Tyler were among the oldest and most revered in the community. While Mrs. Prescott-Tyler was one of Rosemont's most sought after social leaders, she was also the most notorious. Leza rarely put much stock in the juicy gossip that floated around Randolph's, but suddenly every scandalous tidbit she'd ever heard about the "merry widow" came to mind. Until that very moment, she didn't connect the Prescott-Tyler name to Maggie's tale of Jared's lost love.

"Lee-za," Peggy stretched out her name as she was prone to do when Leza was preoccupied. "It's time to get the girls lined up for the intro." When she didn't respond, Peggy strained over Leza's shoulder to peer through the curtain, too. "Hey," she said, "isn't that your headache?"

Leza snapped the curtains together, but not before seeing Marianne take Jared's arm and smile adoringly up at him. Turning on her heel, Leza clutched her clipboard to her breast and shouldered her way through the crowd of chattering, giggling, nervous candidates for Rose Queen.

Peggy finally caught up with her. "You're crazy if you let that air-headed society fluff get her claws into that gorgeous hunk of man."

"It's none of my concern who Jared sees."

"Say what you will, but I saw you two together this morning—"

Leza stopped and whirled around abruptly. "Peggy, I have more important things on my mind tonight." Leza rarely snapped at anyone, and it stunned them both.

Leza wanted to apologize, but knew that if she did Peggy wouldn't let it drop. She turned to leave, but Peggy laid a restraining hand on her arm.

"I wouldn't get too far away from the stage, if I were you."

Before Leza could ask what Peggy meant, Mrs. Tyler's voice, amplified from onstage, caught her attention.

". . . appreciate each and every one of our patrons and their generous donations to the pageant, but each year the committee acknowledges one individual whose contributions of time and support . . ."

Leza's eyes widened. "Peg-gy," she unconsciously borrowed her friend's name-stretching habit. "I'm going to kill you."

"Right here?" Peggy asked with her most engaging smile. "Or out there in front of witnesses?"

"You could have at least warned me."

"And missed that look on your face?"

In a gesture that clearly said just-look-at-me, Leza raised her arms out to each side. Her loose-fitting blouse and her most comfortable faded jeans were ideal for her backstage duties, but they were hardly appropriate for accepting Rosemont's show of gratitude before a capacity crowd of two hundred. "I'm hardly dressed for—"

". . . Please help us thank Miss Leza Colletti . . ."

"You're on." Peggy gave Leza a none-too-gentle shove through the curtains.

Leza absolutely hated anything that put her in the limelight. But the minute she stepped before the elite of Rosemont, she straightened her back, squared her shoulders, and accepted two dozen long-stemmed yellow roses and a kiss on the cheek from Mrs. Tyler without a hint of her discomfort. When the applause quieted, she even managed a sincere thank you to the committee for placing their trust in her, and then for allowing her the freedom to do the job as she saw fit. The only time she faltered was when her eyes met Jared's. And he was obviously as stunned to see her on stage as she was to be there.

The last thing Jared expected this evening was to hear the name Leza Colletti announced over the PA system. When he looked up to see her step from backstage, he couldn't have expressed his thoughts in words—not even if someone had been holding a gun to his head. Dressed in a baggy shirt and faded Levi's, she was without a doubt the most beautiful woman in the room.

Unbidden, everything that had passed between them earlier in the day swept through his mind. He remembered their brief encounter at Randolph's that morning and the look on her face when she'd turned to face him. At the time, he hadn't been able to put a finger on her expression. But knowing what he now knew, he recognized it as a mixture of happiness to see him and dread that he had found her.

Later, when he'd trailed her to her apartment—her brother's apartment—he had come on like a macho jerk. No, he amended the thought immediately, he had behaved more like a jealous, scorned lover. In an unconscious gesture, he raked his fingers through his hair.

Damn, what a fool he'd been. She hadn't run away from him, left his bed, to marry Colletti. He was her brother, for pity's sake! No wonder she had been so confused and defensive.

He felt sick at heart when he recalled the things he had said in the heat of the moment. Deep down inside he suspected that she hadn't told Colletti about the assault—or about her involvement with him—and he had blurted it all out callously, intentionally wanting to strike back, to hurt as he'd been hurt.

In less than a heartbeat, the memories filled his mind: the confrontation with Colletti, Leza crumpling to the floor, the argument between her brother and himself when Colletti insisted that he leave. More confused than ever, he left only after Colletti agreed to meet with him after work. The best place for privacy, they decided quickly, was Jared's office.

That meeting, as expected, started off in a heated exchange, but both men calmed down when it became evident that they were getting no place fast. Colletti was pretty tight-lipped in the beginning. Hell, Jared thought, again ruffling his hair, how could he blame him? All Colletti had seen of Jared was his anger and his hostility. It took some doing, but he finally convinced Colletti that he wasn't a threat to his sister. Once that was established, Colletti seemed more inclined to talk.

Starting with her relationship with their parents, her ex-husband, and himself, Colletti spared no detail in explaining how Leza's life had been pretty much dictated by what others wanted for her. One day she'd simply had enough and ended what outsiders considered a good marriage. From the things Colletti said, Jared had to agree with him that Donald St. Clair had been nothing more than an insensitive prig. Colletti's emotions for his family ran deep. It showed when he touched on his niece's tragic death, and how Leza had fallen apart, then pulled it all together to take on a new job so far from her home.

Still, the part that really got to Jared was Colletti's explanation for her leaving Summerset so abruptly. When Colletti accused him of taking advantage of Leza's situation, of seducing her at a time when she was most vulnerable and then snubbing her the next morning, Jared was more than a little stunned. That's when it dawned on him. Jake.

Of course—how had he been so stupid? He hadn't seen Leza again after leaving her room, so it had to have been Jake she'd seen—Jake who snubbed her and rode away.

Thinking back, Jared realized that although he remembered mentioning having a brother, he'd never actually said that they were identical twins. Obviously, no one else had either.

God, what must have gone through her mind? In her fragile state, it must have seemed as if he had been having misgivings about their night together. It all made sense, especially now that he knew what kind of husband St. Clair had been.

If only he'd talked to her when he'd first tracked her down. But no, like the hothead he'd always been, he simply jumped to the conclusion that since her name was now Colletti, she had run away and married another man.

His life hadn't been the same since Leza had come into it, and he'd been miserable without her. He didn't care what he had to do, but he had to talk to her, had to get her alone . . .

A gentle touch on his arm drew him back to the present.

"Have I thanked you properly for coming to my rescue tonight, Jared?" Marianne's honey-sweet voice finally broke the spell that Leza's unexpected appearance had cast over him. Only when Leza slipped out of sight through the curtains did he force his attention to Marianne.

"You should know better than anyone how hard it is to say no to your mother-in-law," Jared said honestly. Marianne looked hurt, but Jared knew her well enough to know that she was only peeved. "I was glad to help out," he added and Marianne's pout turned into a vibrant smile.

"It was important to my Vanna for me to be here

tonight.'' She virtually beamed. ''She's favored to win, you know.''

The years had been more than kind to Marianne. She was even more beautiful than the day they'd planned to be married, but as Jared studied her he found it hard to believe that he had ever truly loved her. Compared to Leza, whose face positively glowed with every emotion she felt, Marianne was a shallow shell of a woman.

''Isn't it wonderful,'' Marianne said, seemingly unaware that Jared wasn't hanging on her every word. ''Twenty years ago I was Rose Queen, and tonight my baby follows in my footsteps.'' Her features suddenly clouded. ''I just couldn't face coming here alone.'' She dabbed daintily at her eyes with a Joy-scented handkerchief she had discreetly taken from her beaded evening bag. ''Van's death was such a shock . . .'' Her words trailed off, her voice cracked with emotion.

More because it was expected than anything else, Jared took her hand and squeezed it tenderly. Shallow and self-centered she might well be, but Jared believed Marianne had loved Vance Tyler as much as she was capable of loving anyone.

Slowly the auditorium lights dimmed, the orchestra came to life, and an hour and half later Vanna Tyler was the reigning Rose Queen of Rosemont.

Minutes later, while clearing Marianne a path through the crowd backstage, Jared found himself unexpectedly face-to-face with Leza. She looked up. The smile on her lips and the glow of excitement in her eyes died when her gaze met his. It wrenched at his gut that just his presence could strip joy right out of her.

People crowded in from all directions—mothers consoling their daughters who had lost, others congratulating Vanna and Marianne on Vanna's victory. Jared momentarily lost sight of Leza, and he knew that it hadn't been by accident. She was surely avoiding him.

When he found her again, she was encircled by six of the pageant contenders. Vanna, the tallest and unmistakenly the most striking of the lot, was crying, hugging Leza, and trying to keep her tiara from slipping off the back of her head—all at the same time.

"Oh, Miss Colletti," he heard Vanna saying above the din of chatter that filled the air. "You were so right about my gown. The blue was the perfect choice for my coloring. The peach would have been all wrong."

To one side, Jared saw Marianne's face flush with color. Evidently the peach had been her suggestion. Jared moved closer, only to be intercepted by Vanna's grandmother.

"Jared." Mrs. Tyler, overcome by the excitement of the occasion, hugged him with genuine affection. "Isn't it wonderful!" Someone called her attention away and again Jared sought Leza in the crowd. Still surrounded by the bevy of beauties, she hadn't been able to make her getaway. He started toward her once more, but Mrs. Tyler stopped him again.

"Come, Jared," she said. "I want you to meet someone." Taking his arm, she ushered him through the knot of people still surrounding Leza. "Miss Colletti," she called, and the small band of weeping, laughing girls parted to allow the older woman's admittance. Jared, well aware of his affect on the opposite sex, graciously accepted the admiring glances of everyone— save one. Leza tried to pretend that she hadn't heard Mrs. Tyler, tried to turn and leave. She didn't quite make it.

Smiling, Leza turned and acknowledged Mrs. Tyler's presence. Still she refused to meet Jared's gaze. Mrs. Tyler seemed not to notice.

"Jared, this is the young woman everyone is raving about." As though she sensed Leza's inclination to flee, Mrs. Tyler looped one plump arm around Leza's waist. "She is an absolute jewel at organizing and overseeing every project we send her way." Jared saw the color begin to stain Leza's fair skin. "I've never seen anyone with such a flair for getting things done," Mrs. Tyler went on. "Her eye for detail is unmatched, and you wouldn't believe the amount of money she saved the planning committee on this coronation." She stopped to take a breath and Jared could have sworn he saw Leza try to inch away.

"Miss Colletti and I met earlier today, Mrs. Tyler. Good to see you again." Almost as a dare, he extended his hand to Leza. The look she sent him could have hammered nails, but she accepted his silent challenge. Her hand was cold and trembled slightly when they touched. He released his grip when she tugged her hand back. "You did an excellent job here tonight." Leza nodded wordlessly.

Jared wasn't about to let her get away now that Mrs. Tyler had unwittingly helped him corner her. "If you'll excuse me, Mrs. Tyler, I have something important to discuss with Miss Colletti." Leza tried to pull away when he took her by the arm and led her away.

"About today," he began, but she cut him off with a weary wave of one hand.

"I don't want to talk now, Jared."

She looked exhausted, and Jared took pity. "I can understand that. You've got your hands full right now." At least they weren't shouting at each other. "I'll wait, and we can go for coffee later."

She shook her head. "No," she said flatly. "You don't understand. There's nothing to talk about. You had your say this morning. I'm all talked out."

It must have been quite a talk she'd had with her brother earlier, Jared thought.

"That's not true, angel." He tried to take her hand.

If he could just tell her what was in his heart, they could work things out.

From nowhere, it seemed, Peggy Johnson appeared to stand behind Leza. Reinforcements, Jared mused, looking into her ice-blue eyes.

"Hey, boss," Peggy said to Leza, "you about ready to finish up here? We need to get this show on the road if we're going to have the Scrabble playoff of the year." Leza's face showed confusion. Peggy rolled her eyes. "Don't tell me you've forgotten that I'm sleeping over because of the painters at my place." Jared caught on before Leza did.

"Oh, yes. Yes, of course," Leza finally said. She wasn't a very good liar, and Jared saw the ploy for what it was—a way to keep him at bay a little longer.

"Ah, there you are," Mrs. Tyler interrupted. "You *are* coming to the reception, aren't you?" she said to Jared, regarding first him, then Leza, and finally Peggy.

"Mr. Sentell is free as a bird tonight," Leza jumped in before he could answer for himself. "Have a wonderful time, and it was good seeing you again."

Under the circumstances, all Jared could do was watch Leza and Peggy make their hasty retreat. "You're forcing me to play dirty, angel," he muttered under his breath.

"Were you speaking to me?" Mrs. Tyler looked confused.

Jared smiled down at her. "No, not exactly." He put his hand on her back and discreetly propelled her in the direction of a small crowd of men standing in a corner. "Now what was it I wanted to ask you about?" He seemed to mull it over for a second or two, then said, "Yes, of course. The Dixieland project. Any luck finding someone to take Simone Jackson's place?"

"No, I'm sorry to say." Mrs. Tyler looked disheartened. "No one wants to be tied down to a job of that size for two and a half months. Where are all the civic-minded patrons when you need them? They're all perfectly willing to shell out any amount of money, but it's quite another story when it comes to actual physical labor and their precious time.''

''I know what you mean.'' Jared feigned just the right degree of exasperation, but was finding it hard to keep a straight face. ''It's a shame there aren't more hard-working individuals like Miss Colletti in Rosemont—''

Mrs. Tyler spun around. ''That's it!'' she cried, her voice rising with excitement. ''Leza Colletti would be perfect. I'm sure Paul would be more than happy to let her help us for such a worthy cause.'' Her eyes were afire with inspiration as they scanned the room. Jared didn't think she'd ever spot Marcrumb standing just a few feet away. ''Paul,'' she called, at last spotting her target. Jared couldn't hold back the smile any longer.

Mission accomplished. Sorry, angel.

TWELVE

Bright and early that following Monday morning, Leza and Peggy sat in Paul Marcrumb's plush office and listened attentively while he and Mrs. Tyler told of the Dixieland Hotel's latest bit of bad luck.

"And so you see, my dear," Mrs. Tyler said to Leza, "we have a December thirty-first deadline looming dangerously near and no one qualified to carry on for us." She glanced from Leza to Peggy. "We're confident that the two of you can take over at this point and pull it all together before the New Year's Eve ball we've scheduled as the last fundraiser of the season." Again her eyes shifted to Leza. "I know it's a last minute plea for help, and I apologize for that, but we had no idea our restoration architect would just up and leave on us." Her eyes flew back to Peggy. "It is a big job, but look at it as a challenge. And remember, too, that Paul will give you all the time off you need and has even arranged for Randolph's to continue to pay both your salaries while you're helping us out," she hurried on. Her eyes darted back and forth between Leza and Peggy so rapidly that Leza was afraid the older woman might get dizzy and fall on the floor at their feet. "And," she stressed the word to regain their attention as they glanced at each other, "the owner has offered you each healthy salaries and a bonus upon completion. There are even living quarters on the second floor at your disposal for the time it takes to finish the job."

From the moment Mrs. Tyler had interrupted Marcrumb to explain the Dixieland's plight, Leza had been intrigued by the notion of being a part of the restoration. After all, how often did one get the opportunity to help restore a hundred-and-five-year-old bawdyhouse? But it was the mention of living quarters that truly piqued her interest.

Steven had become increasingly hard to live with since learning of the rape. A day hadn't passed that he didn't press her to go to the authorities and file a report. And that was something she still couldn't bring herself to do. She had to get out from under his roof before irreparable damage was done to their relationship. Each morning she pored over the classified ads and made countless telephone calls, only to learn that not one acceptable apartment would be available until mid-January. Her name was on every waiting list in town. Although it rankled her that Bob Weber would be taking over her responsibilities during her absence from Randolph's, Leza knew that this project was a godsend.

"Mrs. Tyler." Leza edged her way into the one-sided conversation. "We'll be glad to help out in any way we can." She glanced at Peggy, who gingerly nodded her agreement. "Just tell us where to start and leave the rest to us."

A visible wave of relief washed over Mrs. Tyler's heavily rouged features, and she hurriedly began to gather the papers strewn on top of Marcrumb's desk. "Everything you need is here," she said, smiling her gratitude and handing the files to Leza. "You'll have *carte blanche* in every way. All the owner asks is that you consult him before making any major changes." She glanced at her watch and her forehead furrowed. "I don't know where he could be. It's not like him to be late—"

At that precise moment, the door opened and Jared strolled nonchalantly toward the center of the room. A sinking sensation filled Leza's stomach and she had the sneaking suspicion that she'd been had.

"Sorry I'm late," Jared said to everyone present, but his smile zeroed in on Leza. "Something unexpected came up."

Mrs. Tyler beamed. "You couldn't have planned it better, Jared. Leza and Peggy just this moment agreed to help us out."

"You don't say," he said, again to everyone in the room, although again his smile extended only to Leza. Obviously he was the owner of the hotel, and it was just as obvious, at least to Leza, that he wasn't at all sorry about being late. She didn't know how or when, but she knew that he was responsible for her being offered this position. It was also highly probable that he'd planned his tardiness to give her time to commit herself before learning that he was involved. How underhanded could one man be?

He made his way across the room and pumped Peggy's hand vigorously. "Good to have you aboard," he said, moving on to shake Leza's hand in the same manner.

"Mr. Sentell," Leza started, but stopped short when he didn't release his grip and smiled smugly down at her.

"Call me Jared," he said, and Leza prayed that no one noticed the seductive note in his voice, or saw the silent challenge twinkling in his eyes. "We'll be spending a lot of time together the next two months."

Leza extricated her hand from his and was considering telling him just where he could shove his job offer when Peggy began nudging her toward the open door. "Guess we'll be on our way. Might as well get a jump on all this reading," Peggy said, neatly nipping Leza's pending protest in the bud.

Leza was fuming inside. How dare he pull such a stunt! "I'll bet you're a marvel at chess," she heard Peggy whisper to Jared as they passed him on their way out.

"Isn't this great!" Peggy said, dancing from one side of the empty hallway to the other. "Two whole months out from under Marcrumb's thumb."

"Why did you do that?" Leza demanded.

"Do what?" Peggy had the audacity to look confused.

"You know damned well what. You deliberately kept me from telling them I'd changed my mind." Leza didn't get angry often, but when she did others knew to back off. Everyone except Peggy.

"Yes, and you should thank me for it instead of biting my head off." Peggy glanced first one way, then the other before dragging Leza into their workshop. Closing the door, she said, "What were you going to tell them? That you changed your mind because working with Jared Sentell scared you spitless? I thought you were made of stronger stuff than that."

Leza felt her facial muscles tense. "Jared doesn't scare me."

Peggy's clear blue eyes suddenly clouded with compassion. "You might as well know," she said. "Steven had to talk to someone. He told me everything." She stopped Leza when she started angrily for the door. "I can imagine how you must feel, but from what I can see, Jared's not the enemy. He's the cavalry."

Leza wasn't really mad that Steven had talked to

Peggy. She was certain that one day Peggy would be her sister-in-law. She was just taken by surprise.

Peggy tugged at Leza to sit down beside her on the sofa. "You two have to talk," she said. "Steven thinks Jared's sincere in his concern for you. The least you can do is let the man tell you his side of the story. This has to be as hard on him as it is on you. Think about it."

It was difficult to find her voice, but when she did, Leza was appalled by the self-pity she heard. "But you didn't see his face that morning . . ."

"You were upset. Maybe you misread him." Peggy took Leza's hand. "Just think about talking with him. He's too good a man to lose over a misunderstanding. The worst that can happen is that you'll find out you were right, and you've already been through that." When Leza didn't answer, Peggy leaned over to look straight into her eyes. "Right?" she prodded.

"Right. I guess." Leza stood, wondering if her smile was as weak as her response. "Now," she said with a heavy sigh. "Let's get over to the Dixieland and see what we've let ourselves in for."

Keeping Jared at arm's length during her first three weeks on the job was easier than Leza ever dreamed. They saw each other almost daily, either at the job site or at his office where they often met to go over the progress of the project. But they both carefully avoided taking that first step that would cross the invisible line separating their private lives from their professional association. Their only close call came early on. Standing together at Jared's desk, going over their lists of materials and suppliers, Leza suggested that they could shave a goodly sum off the proposed budget simply by using local merchants instead of out-of-state vendors.

Jared appeared to be listening with interest, but when her hand inadvertently touched his, he bristled and blurted out, "Just order what you need, and I'll worry about paying for it."

Leza had been startled by his brusque remark. "That's not the point," she returned hotly. "Why go out of the area when we have perfectly qualified businesses right here in Rosemont. People who can not only do the job, but need the work? Look," she persisted, shoving her predecessor's notes under his nose. "Both these companies are in Boston. I'm sure Miss Jackson is a competent restoration architect, and she probably deals with these people all the time, but I can get the same patterns from Shreveport for two dollars less per roll. The chandeliers are right here in town at Lighting World." She flipped through the file. "And the picture frames and antiques," she said, throwing her hands up in exasperation, "are coming all the way from Virginia. Why not contract Micah Blackstone to make those frames for us? His work is exceptional, all done by hand, and it's common knowledge that he could use the money since his wife's stroke last month." Even though she saw that she'd made her point, she pressed the issue. "And Martha Greerson has the best selection of period pieces I've ever seen. Just think of the extra freight charges we'll be saving. We could put that money to other use—"

"All right." Jared held up one hand to silence her. "You've made your point. I wasn't aware so much had been ordered from out of state."

"Doesn't look like you were aware of too much at all," Leza muttered under her breath. She was taken aback when Jared seized her by one arm and spun her around to face him.

"I've had other things on my mind lately," he all but growled.

"You two want to be alone."

Both had forgotten about Peggy and were surprised

by the sound of her voice. Thankfully Jared's intercom buzzed, saving them both further embarrassment.

"Yes?" Jared answered, turning his back to Leza while she quickly gathered the papers strewn across his desk and motioned to Peggy that they were leaving.

"Mack's been waiting for quite some time. He says it's important," Lis's voice broke the silence in the room.

Jared looked relieved. "Send him in, Lis."

No sooner had he said the words, than the door opened. Without a glance, Leza swept past the tall man.

"Boy," Peggy said when they reached the bank of elevators outside Jared's office. "You certainly have a way with men." Leza glared at her, and Peggy just grinned back. "You had one looking at you like he didn't know whether to kiss you or wring your neck, and the other one like he'd seen a ghost?"

"Other one?"

Peggy rolled her eyes toward the ceiling. "God, you are in a bad way. The hunk you nearly knocked over sprinting out of Jared's office?"

All Leza remembered seeing was a dark-blue business suit. "Let's go see Mr. Blackstone and get his ideas on the frames for the Wall of Fame," she said distractedly as the elevator door whooshed open.

That had been over two weeks ago, and each evening after Peggy and the other workers had gone for the day, Leza half expected to see Jared at the door of her new, albeit temporary, home at the Dixieland. But he hadn't shown up, hadn't called, hadn't made any overture that could possibly be construed as anything other than strictly professional. That worried her somehow. Did he have some other dirty trick up his sleeve, or had he simply decided she wasn't worth the trouble?

Leza stood alone on the wide front gallery of the Dixieland Hotel, a screwdriver in her right hand. Peggy, whose small efficiency apartment was just over six blocks away, had been gone well over two hours, but Leza was still hard at work. She stepped back to read the plaque she'd just attached to the freshly painted wall beside the front entry. It read:

DIXIELAND HOTEL MUSEUM

Built circa 1885, this fine example of Greek Revival architecture served for two decades as the private residence for the Will Prescott, Esq. family. It fell upon hard times in the late 1920s when it was purchased by Sarah Goodsong. Taking advantage of the influx of oil field workers during Rosemont's oil boom years, Miss Goodsong renamed the Prescott house and operated it as a bordello until the citizens of Rosemont closed its doors in 1956. After years of neglect, when the building and adjoining twelve acres fell into a state of decay, the property was purchased by an anonymous benefactor, who, with the help of the Rosemont Historical Society, restored it to reflect its past splendor.

An anonymous benefactor. Leza read the words again. It was just like Jared to take up the cause, and then to refuse any of the credit. He was a complex man, a man of many faces, a man who elicited varied and intense emotions from her.

"Stop it!" she said aloud, angry with herself for allowing him to slip into her thoughts so easily. It had taken some doing, but over the weeks she'd finally dissuaded Peggy from bringing his name into every conversation, and now she was doing it herself.

A cold blast of late November wind whistled through the columns of the majestic old building, reminding

Leza that it would be dark in less than an hour. She had a thousand things to do tonight before she could call her time her own.

The grandfather clock in the hall chimed softly nine times. Leza glanced up to see that she'd been working steadily for almost three hours. She straightened, stretching back muscles that were stiff and cramped from tedious hours of unpacking and logging in seven boxes of fine china and silver that would one day grace the huge mahogany table in the formal dining room. Now that she had taken a breather, she realized she hadn't eaten a bite since lunch, when Peggy had made a fast trip to the nearest diner. In the sawdust-covered kitchen of the Dixieland Hotel, they'd feasted on chicken with sweet-and-sour sauce, french fries with catsup, and ice-cold ice tea. But that had been over nine hours ago, and she was famished.

Just as she started up the stairs to her living quarters, there was a knock at the door. She wasn't expecting anyone. Steven, who usually stopped by after work to see if she needed any help, was bowling tonight, and Peggy would just use her key. There was only one other person who would have the nerve to show up without calling first. She didn't want to answer, but when there was a second, more insistent knock, she knew it was useless to wish him away.

"Stop being such a coward," she scolded herself, finally forcing her feet toward the front door. "Just get it over with."

The first thing she saw was Jared's face, smiling a bit stiffly, but it was the same smile she'd dreamed of for months. Then her gaze fell to his hands. Stacked in a neat pile on top of a large pizza box was a large box of chocolates, a bottle of Chianti, and a dozen white roses.

His voice was every bit as tentative as his smile when

he spoke. "I didn't know if I could ply you with wine or chocolates," he said with that wonderful heart stopper of a grin. "Or if you were a sucker for flowers, but I wasn't taking any chances." He indicated the pizza. Leza saw that he was as uncertain as she was about this particular visit. An awkward silence filled the space between them until Jared broke it. "Am I coming in, or do I eat this damned thing alone in my car?"

The ice was broken and Leza felt the tension draining from her. She laughed softly and stepped back to let him in. "I'll get the plates and glasses," she said just as she realized that there wasn't an empty place to be seen. She'd been a very busy girl tonight unpacking crates and checking invoices against purchase orders. Even the kitchen, the only room on the ground floor that had been empty earlier, had been turned into a storage area since lunch. It would be an exercise in futility trying to find a comfortable spot amidst packing crates, sawdust and—Hoover darted from the kitchen in hot pursuit of a tiny gray mouse—varmints.

"I think we'd be more comfortable upstairs," she said, leading the way up the flight of stairs that led to her tiny apartment.

She saw by the look on Jared's face that he approved of what she'd done with the small but cozy rooms that would eventually house the curator of the museum. It hadn't looked like much when she'd first moved in. Other than a fresh coat of paint and a new Ben Franklin fireplace, it had lacked any real warmth or personality. Diligently she had worked in her spare time, adding her own personal touches that made it home.

White wicker furniture—a love seat and two chairs covered with cheery yellow and green floral cushions— was the focus of the room. But the splashes of greenery— ferns and ivies—hanging from the ceiling and scattered around lent the room its real charm.

Now, standing next to Jared in the doorway, the room seemed even smaller. Still a bit nervous, she left the door open as she invited him in. "Make yourself comfortable," she told him on her way to the kitchen. When she returned with plates, glasses, and napkins, she found Jared sitting in one of the chairs, the pizza box open on the cocktail table before him.

He stared at the contents with a look she couldn't quite describe. Then, without glancing up when she sat across from him on the love seat, he said in a manner that clearly showed his disbelief, "People *really* eat this stuff." His eyes were still glued on the pizza. "And *like* it." He shook his head. "It looks like—" Clearly trying to lighten the mood, he forced a shudder of revulsion. "Never mind what it looks like."

Again, she laughed. Although he looked a bit out of place in the overtly feminine surroundings, Leza was struck by how stunningly masculine he was. She couldn't quite decide if she liked him better dressed in a tailored three-piece business suit, or as he was now, in snug button-up Levi's and a form-fitting western shirt. It was a toss up, she decided, and consciously reined in her wayward thoughts.

"I was just going to make myself a sandwich," she offered, stopping when he shook his head in resignation.

"No," he said, his tone as solemn as his face. "We all have to make sacrifices." He picked up one of the larger slices and took an experimental bite.

The host of expressions that played across his face while he chewed and swallowed was interesting, to say the least. But when he grinned, she knew that pizza had made another conquest.

"Not bad," he conceded between bites, and handed her a slice. "Not bad at all." A slice or two later, he uncorked the wine and poured them each a glass. "Now for the wine plying," he said with one villainously arched eyebrow. He lowered it sheepishly when she raised her own brow back at him. It suddenly seemed as if they had gone back in time, that they were again the same two people at Summerset who had learned to share each other's moods, each other's thoughts.

Jared's eyes held hers and what she saw in them made her insides turn to jelly. He wanted her. Tonight. Now. And what was worse, no matter what had passed between them, she wanted him every bit as much.

The dripping of the faucet in the kitchen became magnified in the quiet of the room, bringing reality crashing back upon them. They each took a sip of the wine, hesitated awkwardly, and took another. After a moment, Jared set his glass aside, then leaned forward and took Leza's.

"We've danced around it long enough, angel."

She wanted to stand and walk around the room, but she didn't. Instead, she took a deep breath and fingered the hem of her sweat shirt. "I know. Where do we start?"

"The morning you ran out on me seems like a logical place to me."

She wasn't sure if he had meant to or not, but his choice of words put her immediately on the defensive. She came to her feet. "Ran out on you?" she said, sarcasm lacing her words. "You can sit there and accuse me of running out on you when—"

"Sit down," Jared interrupted, then repeated himself more gently. "Just sit down, Leza. I have something to show you." He seemed so sincere that she did as he asked while he searched each pocket of the Dallas Cowboys windbreaker he'd discarded earlier. At last he found what he was looking for. "Look at this," he said, rounding the cocktail table to sit so close to her that she could smell his cologne.

It was a snapshot of a group of people on what Leza

recognized as the back steps of Jared's house. Maggie, surrounded by several children, all boys, was spooning homemade ice cream into bowls while Jared cuddled a toddler on his lap. An attractive younger woman was at Maggie's side, and next to her stood Brad and—Jared?

She did a quick double take. Confused, she glanced up at Jared, then back at the photo. Aside from the khaki uniform and the handgun strapped to his hip, the other man was the spitting image of Jared.

"Brother?" she asked, the puzzlement inside her finding its way into her voice.

Jared nodded. "Not just my brother. My identical twin."

A lump began to form in her throat as the impact of what she had just learned hit her. It hadn't been Jared she'd seen that morning. Unable to believe it, she looked at the snapshot again. From a distance, anyone who didn't know would easily have made the same mistake. It was a few seconds before she could speak. "I thought—" She couldn't go on.

"Steven told me what you thought." He took her hand and squeezed it ever so slightly. "It all made sense once I realized that as often as I'd mentioned Jake, I'd never told you we were twins. I still can't believe Maggie didn't tell you."

For the first time in months, the tightness in Leza's chest began to ease, really ease. It had all been a mistake. Jared hadn't been put off by her aggressive behavior the night they'd made love, hadn't snubbed her the next morning when she'd called out to him. It had been Jake.

She wanted to laugh. She wanted to cry. She wanted Jared to hold her and never let her go. But then she remembered the day he'd shown up at Randolph's, and later at Steven's apartment. Why had he been so cold, treated her—and Steven—so harshly?

"That explains that," she said, standing and clasping her hands in front of her while she put some distance between them. But there were still some things she had to know, and she didn't trust herself to think clearly with Jared sitting so close, smelling so wonderful. "But it doesn't tell me why you treated my brother like he was some sort of monster, like you *wanted* to hurt . . ." Her words trailed off, and she turned on him. "What were you thinking, Jared, when you barged in and told Steven about the rape?" She watched him shove his fingers through his dark hair, stand, and ram his hands into his pockets.

"I thought . . ." he began, pausing to ruffle his hair again.

"You thought what, Jared?" He'd put her through hell that day, and she wasn't going to make it easy for him now. "Go on, say it!"

"I thought—dammit, Leza—it sounds so ridiculous now."

"Try sounding ridiculous, then. I want to hear it from you. Tell me," she demanded again.

"All right." He glared at her from across the room. "I thought you'd used me, slept with me to see if you could go to him and not have to worry about falling to pieces when he touched you."

"He?" This was getting better all the time. "Who?"

"Him!" Jared shouted, turning crimson. "Steven."

"My brother?" Leza sputtered, suppressing a giggle of pure astonishment.

"I didn't know he was your brother." He was pacing now. "Hell, his name is Colletti. Yours was St. Clair, now it's Colletti." He wouldn't have any hair left if he kept plowing through it like that. "You were as cold as that bottle of wine that day at his apartment. You were wearing that damned man's robe, and then there was *that*!" He stopped pacing and pointed at her copy of the photo of Steven and herself. "What was I supposed to think? To someone who didn't know you two were brother and sister, it looks like one happily married couple."

It all made sense now, and it wasn't funny anymore. Her past experience with Don had fanned the flames of her guilt for being the sexual aggressor with Jared. And when it appeared that Jared had been disappointed in her afterward, she had been devastated and had taken the coward's way out. Jared, unaware of the turmoil roiling within her, had been just as devastated by what had to have seemed like her desertion.

Taking pity on him, Leza rushed to him and laid her head against the soft cotton of his shirt. The moment his arms tightened around her, she knew how much she wanted him, had always wanted him.

She heard his heart rate accelerate beneath her ear. Each strong and rhythmic beat filled her with hope for what was yet to be and took away the pain of yesterday. She felt a moment of loss when he released her, then his lips took hers in a kiss so full of want and need that it snatched her breath away.

His tongue demanded entrance, and her lips opened for him. Sensations she'd only read about, dreamed of, bombarded her when he moaned her name aloud. His hand moved up to cup the back of her head. His fingers laced through her hair to hold her immobile while his lips and tongue, hungry and wild, devoured hers.

It was impossible to think rationally, but through it all one thing was crystal clear. Too much time had been wasted through stupid misunderstandings.

She arched against him, her body telling him more clearly than words that this was their time.

Boldly, she dropped one hand to cup his buttock before tugging his shirttail free. Sliding both hands beneath his shirt, she let them roam freely across the muscled expanse of his back, then leisurely back up the length of his torso. With unsteady fingers, she loosened each button on his shirt. It opened, and she pressed her cheek against the solid wall of his chest. He smelled of after-shave and soap and outdoors. Masculine smells, nice smells that mixed with his own scent to inflame her senses as surely, as strongly, as the most potent aphrodisiac. She heard his quick intake of breath when her lips lightly grazed one nipple.

"The floor's starting to look mighty good," Jared said jaggedly.

"Not when there's a perfectly good bed in the next room." Taking his hand, she led him through the door to her bedroom.

"That's not a bed," he said, eyeing her pillow covered daybed skeptically. To someone who was used to having a king-size bed all to himself, the idea of two people sharing something this size must have seemed ludicrous.

"Don't be such a snob," she chided through a throaty laugh.

"I'm not being a snob." he quickly defended himself. "That thing's hardly big enough for one person, much less two."

With unshakable confidence, Leza caressed his well-defined jaw. "Where there's a will, there's a way. Besides," she said with a twinkle in her eye, "as someone whose opinion I greatly respect once told me, we all have to make sacrifices."

He muttered something she didn't quite catch as he took her hand. In a matter of seconds, every fluffy, frilly pillow on the bed wound up on the floor, along with their clothes.

When they at last lay together, Jared covered her body with his. She loved the texture of his skin, the feel of his weight on top of her. Braced on his elbows, he buried his hands in her hair and lowered his mouth to hers. He kissed her slowly, thoroughly, then stopped to trail feather kisses across her forehead, her nose, her eyelids. His breathing had grown heavier, and when he looked down at her, there was an uneasy moment when his eyes held hers.

"There are no ghosts, Jared. Only you and me."

Even as she assured him, she felt tremors coursing through her. He smiled down at her, then rolled to one side to caress first one full breast, then the other. He seemed to sense that she wasn't trembling with fear, but rather with expectation and need. His touch was electrifying, and like so many live wires, her senses sprang to life.

Her hands began an exploration of their own, and the hair on his chest teased the sensitive tips of her fingers.

"Oh, yes, angel," he breathed, stroking his hand down the length of her spine. "Touch me." His head fell back when her lips grazed his throat. "Taste me." With a boldness she hadn't known she possessed, she began to scatter myriad butterfly kisses down the length of his torso. Briefly, she stopped to suckle each male nipple lightly before venturing lower. That certain part of him surged with life beneath her lips. He moaned aloud, and pulled her up and under him.

"God, Leza, I need to be inside you."

Suddenly, urgently, his mouth crushed her, and she knew that all this time he had been restraining himself. It was time to let him lead the way.

Sliding one hand beneath her, he lifted her and took her with a desperation that was both fierce and demanding. Together they moved in a quickening rhythm to the pinnacle of their passion. "Now, Leza," he whispered hoarsely against her ear, and for only the third time in her life, the painful tightening in Leza's loins suddenly broke and poured from her. Totally spent, she was unable to move or speak while Jared held her tightly and absorbed her tremors with his own body. When at last she felt his weight sag on top of her, she wrapped her arms tightly around him. She was unaware of the passage of time until he eased her to lay alongside him.

Cuddled with her head on his shoulder, Leza would have been content to lie there beside him for eternity. She glanced up to see him smiling in the darkness. The light from the other room made it possible for her to see every detail of his profile, including that adorable lone dimple.

Idly, she let her hand journey across his chest. "Why can't you have two dimples like everyone else?" she asked, lightly tracing the firm set of his jaw.

"I do," he said with a lazy smile. His breathing still hadn't returned to normal, and she felt her pulse quicken at the husky quality his voice held.

She turned his face so she could see the opposite cheek. "No, you don't."

He just nodded, and she was fascinated by the gentle rise and fall of his chest.

"Where?" she wanted to know.

He turned his head and graced her with said dimple once again. "Don't tell me you missed it." They both laughed and he pulled her back into the crook of his arm.

Leza felt a rush of warmth spreading through her again when his hand moved up and down the length of her arm. She snuggled closer and whispered softly against his throat, "You make me feel so much." Her arms wound around his neck, pulled his head down to hers.

"And you make me feel like I'm walking on sunshine."

She couldn't help smiling against his lips.

"What's so funny?"

"Nothing," she breathed, reluctant to release him for

even a second. "It's just that that's what my father calls me. Sunshine."

That made Jared laugh. "Leave it to me to remind you of your father at a time like this."

"Nothing about you reminds me of my father." She nuzzled her face against the hollow of his neck, memorizing the smell, the taste of him. "Or anyone else in my family."

"No more talk of families," he said, his mouth covering hers again, his hands beginning a slow exploration of her back, her hips. Suddenly he embraced her tightly, urgently, then rolled her onto her back. None to gently, he nudged her legs apart to slip between them. Again he kissed her, this time almost violently. "God help us both if you ever leave me again." If she heard the threat in his words, she ignored them and gave herself over to the magic his body performed on hers.

THIRTEEN

From the moment Jared revealed his misconceptions about Steven and explained about Jake, Leza's life made a complete turnaround. No longer was she driven almost to the point of exhaustion by her work. As difficult as it could be at times, being in charge of the Dixieland project was so much fun that she almost felt guilty for taking her weekly paycheck. Almost.

It was her last night in her second-story quarters at the Dixieland, and she was filled with excitement as she dressed for the New Year's Eve costume ball scheduled to start in less than an hour. Tonight's festivities were not only bringing one chapter of her life to a close, but starting another. At morning's light she was moving into her very own little house on Easy Street.

Easy Street. She smiled, liking the sound of it. By no stretch of the imagination could the phrase rolling in dough be used to describe her, but the extra salary and the bonus she earned from the Rosemont Historical Society helped her finance a prime piece of real estate Jared had helped her locate.

Just the thought of Jared produced its usual rush of warmth inside her. She hugged it to herself, along with the memories of the past two months.

She hadn't thought anything could be as special as spending Thanksgiving with Jared. Then Christmas came and she realized that where he was concerned, her happiness knew no bounds. They spent Christmas Eve with Steven and her parents, who had driven in from Odessa for the holiday, then exchanged their gifts in private back at her place. Christmas Day with Jake and his growing family had been hectic, to say the least. But Becky, who was expecting her fifth child in early spring, welcomed Leza into Sentell clan with a sisterly hug and the promise of sharing her best recipes. Leza fit right in, just as Jared had with her family. Perversely, though, she refused to acknowledge all she had to be grateful for because, in a childlike way, she was afraid of jinxing what she still considered her tentative relationship with Jared.

If it bothered her that Jared hadn't made a verbal commitment to her, she didn't dwell on it. The time they had together was far too special for her to let her insecurities plague her. Especially when she suspected that privately Jared was still dealing with insecurities of his own.

God help us if you ever leave me again. She remembered the quiet desperation in his words, and her heart ached for him. Although there had been no declarations of undying love between them, Leza knew his feelings for her ran deep. She felt certain that old wounds and old memories kept him from making the commitment she secretly craved.

While she continued to dress, she said a quick, silent prayer that tonight would also be the beginning of a new chapter in their relationship.

With a great deal of wriggling and twisting, she

finally secured the fastener at the back of her dress, then stepped back and eyed her reflection in the full-length mirror. Red was definitely her color, and the satin fabric of the form-fitting, strapless gown swished about her ankles like whispers in the night. She remembered the day she and Peggy had stumbled across a dusty old trunk stored in the attic, and their delight in finding it packed to the rim with many of Sarah Goodsong's personal belongings.

It was common knowledge that Leza, with Peggy's help, had shouldered most of the responsibility of organizing the gala grand opening affair. Upon learning of their discovery, Mrs. Tyler was quick to insist that Leza preside as hostess on New Year's Eve. And what better costume for the hostess than one of the infamous madam's own gowns?

Now that Leza saw herself decked out in the finery of the 1930s, she had to admit that it hadn't been a bad idea. With only minor alterations, the gown fit like it had been custom made for her. She made several graceful pirouettes, laughing and taking care not to step on Hoover, who was busy with a feline dance of her own at Leza's hemline.

Yes, she vowed with one last look in the mirror, it was up to her to heal Jared's wounds, erase his bad memories with the love she would share with no one except him.

Downstairs, the doorbell rang, and Leza smiled at her reflection. Jared had promised to pick up the extra case of champagne the liquor store had failed to deliver earlier, and he was right on time.

"Door's open," she called, gathering the crimson feather boa that completed her costume and casually draping it around her bare shoulders. Her reflection caught her eye again, and she blushed at the swell of flesh brimming over the decolletage. She might well be a passable facsimile of Sarah Goodsong, but *this* woman's affections belonged to one man, and one man alone.

"I'll be right down, Jared." Eager to greet him in private before the other invited guests arrived, she hurriedly opened the jewelry case she'd also found in the attic. It took a few seconds to locate the ruby-studded earrings she was certain Sarah had in mind when she purchased this particular dress. She slipped them through her earlobes, then reached for the matching necklace. She was so busy fumbling with the clasp that she didn't notice how peculiarly Hoover had started to behave until she heard a loud hissing noise. She glanced to her left to find the animal backed into the corner, her back arched high in the air, her teeth bared in what appeared to be a snarl. Leza had never known the cat to react to anything so violently, and the sight sent a chill through her. Suddenly, she felt fingertips securing the clasp at the nape of her neck. Her only thought was that Jared would never take the chance of scaring her like this. She whirled around and her heart literally skipped a beat.

"No," she heard herself gasp. It couldn't be *him*. If there was a God in heaven, He wouldn't allow this to happen. Even as she prayed, she knew that no matter how long she lived, she would never forget his face—or what he'd done to her.

"I see you remember me," Tom Maxwell said so softly that Leza couldn't be certain he was real. But his smile was real enough, and it mocked her as his eyes slid over the length of her. "Nice dress," he said with the exact degree of huskiness intended to add insult to the compliment. "And very appropriate."

Leza, reacting purely from instinct, tried to dart past him but Maxwell was faster, and easily blocked her path. "Sorry," he said without a trace of apology.

"We have to talk before Jared and the others get here."
His hand locked around her wrist.

Leza jerked free, and noticed for the first time that he
was dressed in formal evening attire. "You . . . know
Jared?" she stammered, remembering that she and Peggy
had addressed the invitations personally. Tom Maxwell's name hadn't been on the guest list.

"You really don't know, do you?" He looked like a
cat toying with a mouse. "I'm Mack Thomasson."

The name sounded familiar, but for a few seconds
she couldn't place it. Then it struck her. Mack Thomasson
was Jared's business associate. Although she had never
met him, she'd heard the name dozens of times.

"But you're Tom—"

"You disappoint me," he interrupted. "Surely you
didn't think I'd tell you my real name."

It was suddenly difficult for her to swallow, even
harder to breathe. She saw his gaze drop to her cleavage, which rose and fell with each quick intake of her
breath. The same neckline she'd found so alluring just
moments ago now made her feel completely undressed,
utterly vulnerable. From some inner reservoir of strength,
she squelched the impulse to cover herself.

"Looks like we have us a real problem here." Although his voice had a pleasant timbre, she heard the
threat in his words.

She jerked her eyes toward the door and prayed that
Jared would miraculously appear. Maxwell simply smiled,
and again she felt chilled to the bone.

He closed the distance between them with one calculated step. "Jared's running late, so I volunteered to
bring the booze for him." He paused, and even in her
state of near panic, Leza sensed that he did so for
effect. He enjoyed exerting his will over others. "So
we could talk." She'd never seen eyes so filled with
. . . what? Anger? Hate?

"Talk?" Nervously Leza rearranged the boa to conceal her bustline. She felt trapped. She wanted out of this room, wanted him out of her home. "We have nothing to talk about."

"We have plenty we have to get straight." He motioned toward the sofa. Stubbornly she refused to sit down. He shrugged, and glanced at his watch. "Have it your way, but you're going to hear me out before the others get here." He started to pace, then stopped himself, as if sensing that he would lose his advantage if he lost his cool. "I've been wondering what you were going to do ever since that day you and your friend almost knocked me over in Jared's office."

Stunned, first by his unexpected appearance and now by this statement, Leza's mind went blank. Then it clicked: Later, in the hall, after she and Jared had argued about ordering supplies from local merchants, Peggy commented on the hunk who looked like he'd seen a ghost.

"I really wasn't surprised that you didn't go to the law," he was saying when she focused back on him. "None of them ever do. Things are different now that you and Jared are so thick." Something akin to fear flickered in his dark eyes before the hate filled glimmer she'd noticed earlier returned. "You just keep your mouth shut and nobody else'll get hurt."

"Keep my mouth shut!" Leza surprised herself by shouting. She didn't like being threatened, but held her tongue when he took another step toward her.

"I don't think you have any idea how things stand, *Miss* Colletti." Something in his tone frightened her. "What do you think Jared's reaction would be if I told him you led me on that night, that you gave me every go-ahead signal a woman knows how to use, then cried rape when things got a little out of hand?" A self-satisfied sneer contorted his handsome features. "Lots of women like it rough, you know."

She shouldn't have been surprised that he was actually threatening to make her look like the guilty party. Hadn't she heard stories from the women in her support group about other rapists using similar tactics in their defense?

"Jared thinks I'm a man of my word, *Miss* Colletti." Again she heard the emphasis on the word Miss. "Who's he going to believe? His indispensable business associate, the devoted friend who saved his life in Vietnam?" There it was again, that hate filled look that made her step back involuntarily. "Or a woman he finds pleasure sleeping with, but hasn't bothered to marry?"

If he'd landed a physical blow, he couldn't have hurt her more. Had Jared discussed their relationship with this animal when he'd never even mentioned their future to her?

"Miss Colletti," a voice called from below. "It's Ellen Linsley with Cockrell's Catering. We're setting up in the kitchen."

Relief washed over Leza and she rushed past Thomasson and out the door.

"You can't run from me all night." His words followed her down the back staircase. She didn't stop until she reached the servant's entrance to the kitchen. There she paused and forced air into her lungs by taking deep breaths.

She had been so in control of her life until just a few minutes ago. What was she to do, and how was she going to make it through this evening with Maxwell—Thomasson—watching her every move?

"Hey, old buddy," she heard Thomasson say in the foyer. "Your best girl and I were thinking about starting this wingding without you." He sounded so carefree. It grated on Leza as she cowered in the hall at the back of the house. She pulled herself erect, intending to check on the progress in the kitchen, when she heard Jared.

"There you go, thinking again," he said in the same jovial tone Mack had used. "What have I told you about that?" There was a brief moment of masculine camaraderie before Jared asked, "Speaking of best girls, where is she?"

No matter how difficult, she had to do something about Thomasson, had to decide the best way to handle him. But tonight wasn't the right time or the right place. With another deep breath, she squared her shoulders, pasted a smile on her face, and took her cue.

"I thought I heard you," she managed, giving Jared a hug and a quick kiss, aware that Thomasson's eyes never left her. As tense as she was, she didn't miss how extraordinarily handsome Jared looked in his black tuxedo, or that his tie and cummerbund matched her gown exactly. "Thanks for getting the champagne here on time," she added, noticing the crate labeled *Henri Marchant* on the baby grand piano where Thomasson obviously had left it.

"I told you, I'm a man of my word," Thomasson said casually, taking the thanks for his. "And I was doing a favor for a friend. Where do you want me to put it?" he asked as if nothing more innocent than social small talk had ever passed between them.

"Just—" She had to stop and try again. "Just give it to Mrs. Linsley in the kitchen."

He picked up the crate, then turned and smiled at Jared. "You're a lucky man, old buddy, but you'd better stay close to her tonight. The way she looks in that dress, I just might try to steal her away from you myself." His gaze dipped again to her cleavage, and the only thing that kept her from recoiling physically was Jared's arm around her waist. Still shaken, but feeling safe and protected by Jared's nearness, she snuggled closer when he pulled her against the hard length of him.

"You'll have to overlook Mack," he said the instant he disappeared into the kitchen. "But he has a point, you know." He loosened his hold, then made a slow, deliberate circle around her. "That's quite a dress you're almost wearing." The gray in his eyes softened as they did only when he looked at her, leaving her totally at his mercy as he took her into his arms and kissed her soundly. "Now *that's* the way you're supposed to greet me."

She clung to him, not wanting to lose the security of his arms around her. His touch never failed to fill her with myriad emotions. But, she wondered, trying to quiet the pounding inside her breast, was it his kiss that made it hard for her to breathe—or the knowledge that the man who'd raped her was in the next room?

An unexpected tremor coursed through her. Jared set, her away from him, and she knew that he had felt it too. He spoke her name and she heard the concern in his voice. Unable to trust herself to look him in the eye, she kept her gaze trained on the pearl buttons of his shirt. She'd come so very far from being the obedient daughter and clinging wife of yesterday. It had taken six long, hard months to become the self-assured woman of today. But at this moment, she wanted nothing more than to blurt out the truth, let Jared take control and make everything all right.

"We can come back later, if you want." The familiar voice came from behind, and Leza turned to see Steven and Peggy standing in the doorway. "Or is this part of the evening's entertainment?" Her brother's grin was nearly as silly looking as her friend's.

Leza said a silent thank you for the interruption. In her moment of weakness, she'd come far too close to laying it all at Jared's feet. This was her problem, she decided, stiffening her spine as well as her resolve. Although she hadn't a clue as to how she was going to handle it, she was the hostess for the evening's festivities, and she would see it through to the bitter end. Mack Thomasson or no.

"It's about time you got here," Leza chided, forcing Mack out of her thoughts and giving Jared one final squeeze before whisking Peggy away from Steven. Peggy was also wearing one of Sarah Goodsong's costumes, a bright blue number that had Steven's eyes glued to her trim figure. Steven, like Jared, looked perfectly natural in his formal wear. "Mrs. Linsley and her crew just arrived. There must be a hundred things we need to do for her."

She didn't realize just how true her words were until she and Peggy began greeting the guests. Neither of them had a second to spare as they made certain everyone was properly introduced, and that everyone had plenty to eat and drink. It would all have been so perfect—except that Mack had an uncanny way of being everywhere, laughing, talking, dancing.

He seemed to know everyone, and no one, not even Jared, appeared to notice the sidelong glances or mocking smiles he threw Leza's way each time he caught her eye.

And no one was immune to his charm: not Becky, not Peggy, not even Mrs. Tyler. The only exception, Leza noticed, was Jared's secretary. It looked to Leza that Lis's retreat each time Mack approached her served only to amuse him. Suddenly Leza felt sick at heart. Had he hurt Lis, too, or did she simply possess well honed instincts where Mack Thomasson was concerned?

If she hadn't had Mack in sight, she would have jerked away from the gentle pressure on her bare shoulder. Instead, she looked up to see Jared smiling down at her. Until that very moment, she hadn't realized she'd been avoiding him as surely and effectively as she'd been avoiding her attacker.

"You can relax, angel," Jared said just as the music started up again. "Things couldn't be going more smoothly. Enjoy yourself," he said waltzing her onto the dance floor. "Enjoy me." He held her closer, and the tension inside her began to evaporate.

So much time had been wasted. So many things had kept them apart. There was no way she could know how it would all work out. But if things turned out badly, she resolved, giving herself over to the feelings Jared's nearness induced, she would at least have this night to remember.

Hiring the musicians, two violinists, a cellist, and a pianist, had been Peggy's idea, and happily Leza saw that their repertoire of tunes from yesteryear were the crowning glory of an already successful evening. The music seemed louder than it really was in the crowded room, and Leza felt it pulsating throughout her body. The melody was familiar, though try as she might, she couldn't put a name to it. Suddenly the refrain jogged a line or two of the lyrics into her mind.

Not for just a hour . . . The violins seemed to sing the words . . . *Not for just a day* . . . The cello and piano joined in . . . *Not for just a year, but* . . .

Jared stopped dancing, and tilted her face up toward his. "Always," he whispered, supplying the title she'd been trying to recall. His lips brushed hers so lightly, so lovingly that she ached inside. She scarcely breathed, so afraid was she of waking and finding it all a dream.

She'd loved his eyes from the first time she saw them—eyes that in times of anger were the color of a cold winter sky, and at more intimate moments darkened to the shade of smoke rising off smouldering ashes. The love she saw shining there now removed all her doubt.

It couldn't have been more perfect. The ball was going as planned; everyone was having a good time. Even Jake, who had sworn he wasn't "getting all fancied up in a danged monkey suit just to go to a highfalutin society shindig" was here. Leza spotted him standing across the room with Becky, who looked like a dream in a cloud of pink chiffon. Granted, Jake hadn't worn a tux, but it was, as he reminded everyone, a costume ball. With his considerable power of persuasion, he'd managed to borrow a turn-of-the-century sheriff's uniform from the Historical Society. Leza saw him put an arm around his pregnant wife, who snuggled closer and smiled lovingly up at him.

For the first time since Amy's death, Leza let herself think of having another child. Jared's baby, a little boy with jet-black hair. How wonderful that would be if only—

She glanced up to see Mack Thomasson leaning casually against the fireplace mantlepiece, laughing and talking with Peggy, and the spell was suddenly shattered. Fear for her friend shot through her as she searched the room for Steven.

She finally located him visiting with a small group of people from the hospital, and she wanted to scream at him for leaving Peggy alone, unprotected. Again she sought out Peggy; all looked well. It took a little doing, but at last Leza reined her emotions under control. She was over-reacting. Peggy was perfectly safe. They were in a room full of people, and surely Mack wasn't stupid enough to make a play for her best friend. Then, as if her attention had called his name, Mack raised his head and looked squarely at Leza. She glanced quickly away, stepping on Jared's toe as she did. She couldn't let Mack see the fear she knew was in her eyes.

"I didn't want to mention it," Jared said, "but you haven't been yourself all evening—"

"I know she's yours, friend," she heard Mack say from behind her. "But how 'bout letting someone else dance with the most beautiful woman in the room?" Something in the way he said the word "woman" sounded sleazy. Leza shouldn't have been surprised that he would have the nerve to approach her again, but if he dared touch her, even as innocently as holding her to dance, she'd lose her mind.

"I have to check with the caterer," she said abruptly, not missing the way Jared's forehead furrowed with puzzlement.

Thankfully the kitchen was empty except for Hoover, who had discovered a splattering of caviar on the floor beneath the sink. Leza was grateful for Hoover's company, and picked her up. There was no telling how much time she'd have alone, so she knew she had to compose herself quickly. With so much going on tonight, she hadn't found a private moment to consider exactly what effect Thomasson's appearance would have on her life.

If she filed a complaint against him, the rape would become a matter of public record. Would she have the strength to go through a trial, to defend herself against Thomasson's accusations that she had been a willing partner that night? What would it do to Steven and her parents? What would it do to Jared?

Until just a few moments ago, she was certain she wouldn't have hesitated to bring Thomasson to justice. But the look in Jared's eyes, the promise in that one word he whispered to her had given her just too much to risk losing.

The fine hair on back of her neck prickled, and she knew Mack was in the room with her. Turning, she found him just inside the door, watching her in her moment of indecision. The only thing separating them was fifteen feet and the kitchen table. Images of him flirting with Peggy flashed like lightning through her brain. Were any of them—Peggy or Lis or Becky or any of the other women here tonight—safe with him on the loose?

"Look," he began, his voice low to keep from carrying to the next room, "I know we got off to a bad start, and I'll take the blame for that. I startled you, but it's important that we settle things between us." He paused, and Leza sensed that he was choosing his words carefully. "For Jared's sake, if for no other reason."

She saw it before he said another word. He was going to use his friendship with Jared to work on her.

"I've known Jared since the tail end of Vietnam, and I know you won't believe it, but I want him to be happy just as much as you do." She started to interrupt, to tell him that nothing he could say would dissuade her from going to the law with her story, but he silenced her with a wave of his hand. "Just let me have my say." He moved closer to the table, but stayed on his side of the room. "I saved his life in that hellhole, and he owes me." She saw him quickly check his hostility, and knew instantly that he had used Jared's sense of obligation to his advantage many times in the past. Mack didn't seem to notice that she was on to him. "I heard all about the hell he went through with his leg, then having Marianne jilt him. Well, you know the story. I just can't stand seeing him hurt by what happened between us when we can work together to protect him."

Leza couldn't believe what he was saying. She wanted to scream at him that nothing had happened between them, that he had raped her. And that he didn't need to protect Jared. Jared needed to be protected from people like him. She had plenty to say, but Thomasson was intent on stating his case first.

"I have a solution, if you'll just listen." He had changed tactics, and there was a note of pleading in his voice now. "Jared's opening a new Gulf Coast division of Sentell Enterprises in Houston. He wants me to be in charge of the entire operation." He began to pace, then stopped to fix her with a look of exasperation. "Don't you see? I'll be over three-hundred miles away, out of your lives for good. I'll see him only twice a year, and only at the office. He'll be happy; you'll be happy; I'll be happy."

That got her. "*You'll* be happy!" She couldn't be quiet a second longer. "And free to hurt anyone else you care to." She stalked to the table and glared at him. This man had reduced her to a quivering mass of nothing once before. She wouldn't allow him to do it again. Until she stood up to him, did something to stop him, she would continue to be his victim.

He must have read the determination in her eyes, in her stance, because she saw his jaw set and his eyes darken ominously. "You'll lose everything," he said in a soft, low growl meant to intimidate her. "And you'll *always* live with the memory that it was your choice."

Always. Jared had promised her always, and the knowledge reinforced her resolve. "I don't think it'll come to that, but it's a chance I'll take to make sure you never hurt another woman."

In a flash, he skirted the table and had her in his grip. "You don't have the guts," he said, shaking her so violently that Hoover broke free and fled, but not before clawing him. Mack ignored the pain and the blood on his hand. "I tell a very convincing story. When I'm through, you'll be lucky to have a job or any friends, much less Jared." He laughed, and the sound was so evil that even with a house full of guests, he frightened her.

From nowhere, Jared tore Mack away from her and

slammed him against the wall. Terrified by the unleashed violence she saw in Jared's face, Leza was powerless to stop him from bouncing Mack repeatedly against the wall. At first, Mack looked like he didn't know what had hit him, but it didn't take long for him to recover. He retaliated by ramming Jared in the stomach, and they both crashed to the floor. They were a flurry of arms and legs. Their angry voices filled the room with loud grunts and unintelligible words.

At first glance, it appeared that they were equal in size and strength, but Jared's rage gave him the edge. Blood flowed freely from Mack's nose and mouth when Jake intervened by pulling Jared off him. Instantly, Mack came up fighting, and Steven stepped in to restrain him.

"What the hell's going on?" Jake demanded.

"Keep out of this, Sentell," Mack warned, wiping the blood from his face. His eyes were dark with fury and riveted to Jared's. "It's personal."

"It's personal, all right," Jared agreed readily enough. One glance at Leza told her he'd heard all he needed to know. "You're just lucky the law's here to step in."

"Come on, old buddy, just because I saw her first—"

Jared grabbed him by the lapels and another scuffle broke out. It took some doing, but soon Jake, with Steven's help, was able to bring order again.

"Everyone back to the room across the hall," Jake barked to the crowd that had gathered in the doorway. He placed his six-foot frame between his brother and Mack, leaving Steven free to go to Leza. Gratefully, she leaned into him for support. He pulled her close to him, and she couldn't hold back the trembling any longer. She heard the words rape and animal and a few others that she blocked out, but when she felt Steven try to leave her side, she heard herself plead, "Stay with me, Steven. Please."

Their words were angrier now, and not even Jake, with his years of police training, could stop Mack from ranting on about how Leza had urged him on that night.

"You'd better let me read you your rights, boy, before you go on." Leza heard the cutting edge in Jake's voice and knew that he was having as hard a time controlling his actions as Jared and Steven.

"I don't need you to read me my goddamn rights," Mack snarled. "I'm walking away from this just like I've walked away from all the other trouble in my life. And I'm sure as hell not going to prison for something she enjoyed as much as I did." His eyes were as glazed as his voice was loud. He glared at Leza. "Women are all alike; you can't trust any of them. Not even your own mother. Just ask me," he raved. "When I was just eighteen, my old lady took my girlfriend's side when I got a little rough with her. But the judge must have seen through their plan, 'cause he gave me the choice: I could go to prison where *they* wanted to send me, or I could join the Army." He laughed. "That's where my life changed. And all because of you, old buddy," he said through a sneer.

Leza no longer feared Mack Thomasson. She pitied him.

"God," Mack yelled at Jared. "Men like you make me sick. Do you have any idea how many times I've used your stupid morals to manipulate you into doing what I wanted? From day one," he answered his own question, laughing to himself. "I didn't save your life in Vietnam, you sap. It was my lucky day when I found you wounded and unconscious in that rice paddy. I pulled you onto my back, not to crawl you out of the line of fire, like they said when they gave me my medal, but to save my ass. I needed protection. And there you were."

Leza had heard all she cared to hear. Obviously so

had Jake. He wrestled Mack around and cuffed his hands behind him. "Jared, you and Steven bring Leza downtown in the morning and I'll take statements from all of you. We'll get the paperwork started so we can lock up this piece of scum." Mack didn't give anybody any more trouble when Jake pulled him toward the back door. "Sleep late," Jake said to Jared. "I'm going to enjoy this."

Across the room Jared looked miles away. All Leza wanted was for him to hold her, but he made no move in her direction.

"I'll let Peggy know what's going on," Steven said, discreetly leaving Jared and Leza alone.

"Why didn't you tell me?" Jared asked.

The last thing Leza wanted right now was to talk, but Jared had been kept in the dark far too long. "I never saw him again after that night until just a few minutes before you got here tonight," she began.

"But he works for me. He's in my office every day. How could you have missed running into each other all these months?"

"I don't know," she said honestly. "He must have been very good, or very lucky, at avoiding me."

"He's been very good at avoiding a lot of things," Jared said with a grim little smile. Leza felt her legs giving way and leaned against the counter for support. She looked up and Jared was at her side. Taking her at last into the circle of his arms, he held her for a few wonderful minutes.

"I know I don't always do things the way you'd like," he started, and she heard the tremor in his voice, "but you have to know I want to be here with you for the good times and the bad." She felt his great body tremble when he placed a kiss on her forehead, heard the uncertainty in his voice when he added, "If you want me."

Leza held tighter to him. "Oh, I

From the other room, the combo [...]
Lang Syne, and Jared laughed alou[...]
Year." His kiss was warm and sweet an[...]
promise of more to come. "I'll ask Lis [...]
shut things down tonight. You look like yo[...] be
in bed." He held out his hand to her.

"There's just one other thing we need to get straight,"
he said at the landing of the back stairs. "About that
little house on Easy Street . . ."

EPILOGUE

Jared sat on the back steps, listening to the sounds of the night that only added to the peacefulness within him. He no longer went to the office everyday. There were some weeks when he didn't go in at all. With Lis's help, he was able to keep up with his workload from his office at home.

The air was fresh and cool against his skin, the fragrance of honeysuckle somehow sweeter than he could ever remember. The thought pleased him when he recalled thinking the same thing every spring night for the past three years.

Leza's laughter tugged his attention to the kitchen, where she and Maggie were gently but firmly rounding up three rambunctious two-year-olds in an attempt to march them off to bed. Swimming and cavorting with his sons at Cold Creek all afternoon had worn him out, so he could well imagine how tired they must be. And Leza—well, she was amazing. Eight months along with twin girls, or so the ultrasound technician had excitedly proclaimed, and not a single complaint out of her all day. He remembered how Leza had teased him about being Superman, a man who in three years had done what it had taken his brother almost seventeen years to do—father five children. But she hadn't let him gloat too long before reminding him that he hadn't accomplished the feat alone. Multiple births were not uncommon on her mother's side of the family.

He felt a smile creep across his face as he continued to watch Adam, Mark, and Lucas each demand and receive his share of his mother's attention. At last, with each child pacified, Leza rose from her kneeling position, stretched backward, and rubbed both sides of her lower back while Maggie scooted the quarrelsome triplets upstairs.

He watched her watching them go, and let his gaze travel the length of her not-so-slender frame. The familiar stirring deep inside of him was a gentle reminder of how empty his life and his house had been before Leza had filled them both with love and laughter. Silently, he thanked his Maker for all that was his.

At that exact moment, Leza turned toward him, the expression on her face telling him that she knew his thoughts were about her. She hung her apron on the peg by the door and turned off the light.

"Want some company?" she asked, taking her usual seat on the step below him and snuggling her back between his thighs. This was their quiet time, their time alone before the nightly ritual of tucking in three sleepy toddlers.

"Always would be nice," he answered, inhaling the sweet, natural smell of her as he nuzzled her neck and gently massaged her rounded belly.

She sighed contentedly and pressed her cheek against his. "Always wouldn't be nearly long enough."